Marigold

Roses & Thorns
Book One

BECCA JAMESON

ACKNOWLEDGMENTS

I have to thank my amazing assistant, Michelle, for all her help plotting this series. It took hours to figure out the overall arc. Bless her for listening to me and helping me flush it out.

PROLOGUE

Ten years ago…

"This sounds so empty and cliché, but I'm so sorry for your loss."

Damon Albertini dropped down into an armchair in his father's study, his hand wrapped around the drink he intended to inhale before pouring another. He gave it a swirl with the tiny red straw, though it hardly mattered. He'd only added a splash of tonic to his Bombay.

"Is there anything I can do?" his best friend, Jagger, asked as he settled into the other armchair. "I can't exactly cook you a meal, and flowers seem a bit extra for a guy."

Damon smiled. "Flowers would be beyond extra, man. I'm glad you didn't show up with any. And I have staff cooking for me, so I won't go hungry." He rubbed the back of his neck and glanced at his father's desk to stare at the piles of paperwork he still had to wade through.

"It looks like you've been working hard to figure out your father's business. Are you planning to follow in his footsteps?"

Jagger asked as he took a sip of his Bombay. He hadn't even added tonic. Smart guy.

Damon shuddered. "Fuck no. My father was living marginally above the law. My mother knew this. That's why she divorced him when I was five. She didn't want me sucked into my father's business, and I won't soil her name by stooping that low."

Jagger winced. "Have you uncovered anything nefarious?" He waved a hand through the air a moment later. "Never mind. Don't answer that. I shouldn't have asked."

Damon chuckled. Jagger worked for the FBI. He wouldn't want to put himself in a position to have to investigate his best friend's livelihood. Damon commended him for his loyalty, but he had no intention of hiding what he'd discovered.

Damon took another heavy drink of Bombay and met Jagger's gaze. "I have a plan, actually."

Jagger stared at him. "Oh?"

"Yes. I've been reading through those files for three days, ever since my father's *heart attack*." Damon rolled his eyes.

"You don't think he died of a heart attack, do you?"

"Oh, I'm sure he did, but I'd bet all his stupid money that heart attack had help."

Jagger took a deep breath. "I figured. You going to ask anyone to look into it?"

"Fuck no. What good would that do?"

"Damon..." Jagger groaned. "Don't tell me you're going to start digging around in his death alone. That's very dangerous."

"Nope. I don't much care about that either. From what I've found, I'm surprised he lived this long. He was under a lot of stress."

Jagger winced. "I assume you've uncovered information that accounts for where all his wealth came from." He hesitated before continuing, "I gotta say, Damon, I'd rather you not tell me."

Damon sighed and swirled his drink again before taking another long sip. "If it were just the money, I'd keep it to myself. I won't play the games my father played. I'm not going to spend my life living on the edge, laundering money to support several mansions and yachts. I will clean up his mess and put the money to good use. However, there's something else I found, and I can't keep quiet about it."

Jagger drew in a breath. "It's going to involve me, isn't it?"

"Yes." Damon held his gaze. "Or your boss. Or your boss's boss. I don't care who."

Jagger nodded slowly. "That big, huh?"

"Depends. How big do you consider human trafficking?"

Jagger gasped, eyes wide. "Your father was trafficking humans?"

Damon shook his head. "No. Never. I've stayed up nearly around the clock, making sure of it. Fuck, at first, I wondered if my mother had been trafficked. I was fucking panicking. But no. However, there's a paper trail. He knows people are trafficking humans."

"Fuck." Jagger ran a hand through his dark hair. "And, you want me to...?"

Damon downed the rest of his drink and leaned forward, putting his elbows on his knees. "The drugs, money laundering, and shit don't ruffle my feathers, but selling women does."

"Damon..." Jagger warned.

Damon met his gaze. Jagger was not going to like his plan. "I'm going to infiltrate all these families my father was doing business with. One by one."

Jagger groaned. "That's fucking dangerous. You'll get killed."

"I won't. My father knew a lot of people. They'll trust me.

I'll make friends. Maybe along the way, someone will hire me to manage their money. I do have a master's in finance." Damon grinned. "Meanwhile, I'll gather information."

"And feed it to me."

"Yes. I find it hard to believe that dozens of Italian families in the Denver area are buying and selling women. I'm betting it's a handful of crime lords. The rest of the families who are living under the law are being manipulated and forced to keep the bigger crime a secret. I bet my father stumbled upon damning information, wasn't willing to keep it to himself, and was murdered for his poor choice."

Jagger glanced at all the files on the desk. "I'm not even going to ask how you've come to this conclusion."

"Good idea. My father isn't the only dead man. His best friend died a week ago."

Jagger winced. "Fuck."

"I'll be talking to his best friend's son later today. He's ten years older than me, so we never knew each other well, but we have something in common. His father had a mysterious stroke."

"Jesus." Jagger ran a hand through his hair. "Do you think he's involved?"

"Not likely. I don't think he's been close to his father for a long time, either. His mother not only divorced his father years ago, and he changed his last name to her maiden name. He owns a chain of fetish clubs called Roses and Thorns. I've been a few times. His businesses are totally legit. He runs a tight ship. Safe, sane, and consensual, or you're out."

Jagger nodded. "That's good. Are you going to ask him to help you?" Jagger questioned.

"No. I'm going to do this on my own."

"You're not asking me to help get you on the payroll, are you?" Jagger inquired.

"Nope. I don't need any fucking money. I'm set for life. I'll sell off my father's properties, buy something comfortable for myself, and put my finance degree to good use. I'll be an inside source, an informant. Totally off the books."

Jagger slowly nodded. "You realize this could take years."

Damon set his glass down and spread his arms to include their surroundings. "I've got nothing but time."

CHAPTER ONE

Three years ago...

"Dad..." Gemma batted her gorgeous eyes at her father. "Please?"

It was hard for Damon to keep a straight face from where he sat behind his boss's desk, his hand on the mouse, his gaze presumably on the monitor. The little imp worked her father hard and often, but the man never backed down.

Salinardi Romano scowled at her from where he sat next to Damon, holding up his hand-written ledger. He'd been in the process of reciting numbers to Damon. "I'd really prefer we turn the clock back to a time when you called me Daddy and enjoyed hanging with me on a Friday night instead of your girlfriends."

Gemma rolled her eyes. "Dad, I'm twenty years old. Not a child anymore. If you took five minutes off work to pay attention, you would know this fact. I'm only asking to go to the movies with my girlfriends. I promise to go there and come straight back. It'll be totally safe."

"No." Romano didn't glance up from his computer. "Have your girlfriends come here. We have a theatre downstairs. Whatever movie you want, ask Marco to arrange it."

"Dad, it's a new release," she whined.

Damon couldn't blame her for wanting some freedom. She was a grown adult. But he silently liked that her father never let her leave the compound. His heart wouldn't be able to take it if he had to worry about her out in the real world.

The woman had no clue...about anything, really. She didn't know what her father did for a living. She had no idea that at least a dozen people would kidnap her in an instant if given the opportunity. She had no idea she was drop-dead gorgeous or that her so-called friends were mostly friends of her father's associates and likely only hung out with her because their fathers insisted.

Though that wasn't entirely true because Gemma was kind and funny and intelligent and had so many other amazing qualities that anyone would be glad to hang out with her.

Romano glanced at his daughter for about half a second. "Since when does that matter? I don't care if the movie comes out next month; Marco can arrange it."

Gemma's shoulders fell, and then she glanced at Damon.

He pretended not to notice in his peripheral vision.

"You can send a bodyguard with us," she insisted. "How about Damon? Surely you don't need him to crunch numbers for you all day. You have a hundred other men on the property. You can spare one guy."

Damon swallowed. *Fuck no.* There wasn't a chance in hell he wanted to be assigned that job. He'd rather guard twenty of Salinardi's men in the middle of an outnumbered drug bust than be sent outside the compound with Gemma and her friends.

It wasn't that he thought it was beneath him. Nor would he mind being forced to spend more time with her. He'd give his right arm to spend more time in her presence. However, she was a walking target. Anything could happen to her. Damon didn't want the responsibility, nor did he want her exposed out in the open like that.

He didn't flinch from his position because he was confident her father wouldn't entertain the idea, mostly because Damon wasn't her personal bodyguard. Instead, he worked for her father, managing his money.

Occasionally, he did get roped into guarding Gemma. Mostly because he was the first man Romano set his eyes on when he needed someone, so he would assign Damon to the task of bodyguard. No way he would do so this afternoon.

"No." Romano met her gaze this time and held it. "Honey, the answer is *no*. Damon has other things to do. He can't be out babysitting you and your friends."

That was true. Damon had climbed the ladder of Romano's inner circle for a year to earn this spot in the man's inner office—a position that afforded him the ability to collect far more information than he'd managed to gather in the previous year of snooping around.

It was comical that Romano still seemed to think his daughter was a child. She was a full-grown woman. Twenty. Even though she was probably as innocent as they came considering her total lack of freedom, she had the body of a fucking goddess.

Her thick dark hair hung in long waves down her back, perfectly styled because Daddy always arranged for her stylist to come to the house. She had gorgeous brown skin that was naturally dark because it rarely saw direct sunlight. She was careful to lather up with sunscreen every time she sat out by the pool.

Pool days were the bane of Damon's existence, especially when he was assigned to guard Gemma and her friends outside. Thank God he wore dark glasses and a suit at all times. The first hid the movement of his eyes. The second hid his constant erection. Somewhat.

Damon couldn't say what any of her girlfriends looked like. He rarely glanced in their direction. Gemma captured every ounce of his attention with her perfect curves, fantastic ass, and high, youthful, full tits.

Yes, he ogled her. He was human, after all. And male. And straight.

He was also there to do a job, so he preferred not to be assigned to watch Gemma. Those days never got him closer to his end goal. The fact that her father often assigned him to Gemma spoke volumes, however. It meant Romano trusted him implicitly, and *that* was an important part of the end goal.

"Daaaddd..." Gemma switched to full-on whining. Damon couldn't blame her. The woman had zero autonomy. She had all the money in the world. Anything she wanted was at her fingertips. She could hire someone to come to the house to do anything she wanted. Change the décor of her suite, outfit her in gorgeous gowns, paint her nails. Massages. Pilates. A personal trainer. She could hire a tutor and learn another language if she wanted—and she had done so. On top of that, Gemma was an accomplished pianist. When she played, her music filled the halls of the estate and made everyone smile, including her father.

Gemma had everything. *Everything.* Except for the freedom to leave the compound. And that had to suck.

Romano was done arguing, and when he was done, everyone knew it. He shot her a glare and pointed at the door. "I'm busy, Gemma. Go find something to do. Play the piano. I love hearing your music throughout the house."

As if she were indeed five, she spun around on her heel and stomped toward the door, taking a moment to shoot daggers at Damon as if he had anything to do with her predicament. As the door slammed shut, Damon flinched subtly, shaking himself out of the trance that woman cast over him when she entered a room.

He'd never once glanced in her direction, so she had no idea he'd noticed her slight, nor the fact that she'd stuck her tongue out at him. She also hadn't known that he'd watched every second of her sexy body as she'd yanked the door open and left the office—from her toned legs to her slim waist to her full tits. She was wearing a sundress that barely covered her ass and no bra. She didn't need one. Her fuck-me, perky tits were perfectly high without support. But every time she did so, she tempted him with her damn pert nipples.

Damon wasn't the only one on staff who noticed, of course. He'd ground his teeth together on more than one occasion when someone on staff stared at her. But Damon had zero claims to her, and he was here to do a fucking job, so he kept his thoughts to himself and forced his hands to remain at his sides instead of popping someone in the nose.

The woman had no idea how fucking appealing she was, and she was far too innocent for the likes of him. She most likely had never heard the term BDSM and wouldn't know a thing about the fetish community.

Nevertheless, Damon itched to pull her over his knees, yank her flirty skirt up, and spank her ass hard. He wouldn't need to pull her panties down because he was well aware that she always wore a thong that left nothing to the imagination.

Hell, her bikini swimsuits were the same. Scraps of material that left her butt cheeks exposed and barely covered her nipples, let alone her breasts.

Gemma Romano was the embodiment of innocence caused by sheltered ignorance, but that didn't stop Damon's mind from roaming in a thousand directions every time he thought about her.

Late at night, he often struggled to sleep, fighting off visions of that sexy goddess naked on her knees in front of him, her hands behind her back, spine straight, eyes downcast. He'd jerked off to the vision, often adding a ball gag to her mouth to teach her a lesson about insolence.

Damon would give just about anything to introduce Gemma to his preferred world, watching her eyes widen with shock as he taught her how to submit to him properly. If she were his, she wouldn't use that sassy tone she often used with her father because he'd discipline her every time until she learned her lesson.

Damon wasn't an asshole. He was a safe player. He always ensured he had consent from his submissives. *Always.* But he'd never had the kind of blank slate Gemma presented. Never been interested in someone with no experience either. He'd never thought of himself as having the patience to train a submissive. He liked to spend a few nights a week at Roses and Thorns, dominating seasoned women who knew what to expect and how to behave.

When he was in Denver long enough to visit Roses and Thorns, he preferred to dominate regulars who knew what they wanted. He hadn't been there for a year. Not since he'd gone undercover to nail Salinardi Romano to the wall.

The reminder of why he was here made him cringe. He was close too. He'd gathered more than enough information to take down Romano and his team for money laundering, drugs, and weapons sales. Damon was still trying to find something more valuable, something that would connect the crime boss to human trafficking.

Damon knew it wasn't going to be easy. Romano handled some of his business by burner phone. And he was careful. Damon usually only caught snippets of hushed conversations. If the man was involved in the human trafficking business, he was fucking careful about keeping it quiet. Damon had yet to secure evidence.

What Damon did know was that Romano had gotten more

and more cautious about his daughter as she grew older and rarely let her leave the compound at all now that she was an adult.

What didn't make sense was why Romano believed anyone he was in contact with would kidnap his child. There was a story behind his overprotectiveness, and it probably involved money. A lot of money. Romano undoubtedly owed someone a large sum of cash, but damned if Damon had found that paper trail yet.

One way or another, Romano was going down. Eventually, Damon would give the FBI enough information for an arrest. If Damon could find even one shred of evidence that Romano was trafficking humans, he wouldn't hesitate to help the FBI take him down for something else just to put him out of business.

It was going to be messy, and Damon cringed every time he worried about what would happen to Gemma after her father was arrested and sent away for life.

"Damon," Romano barked.

Damon shifted his gaze toward the man who fancied himself his boss. "Sir?"

Romano ripped a piece of paper off the notepad in front of him and held it out. "Please go pick up the damn movie my daughter wants to see. It's apparently not available as a download, but there's a hard copy at this address."

Damon inhaled slowly as he reached to take the paper out of Romano's hand. "Yes, Sir." He was a mix of emotions as he headed for the door. He really hated being sent to do such mundane tasks, but he did like to do nice things for Gemma. That woman really got the short end of the stick for a spoiled rich girl.

Damon had to hand it to his boss. For a ruthless drug and weapons dealer with plenty of blood on his hands, he loved his daughter dearly and went out of his way to please her.

Damon also couldn't blame Romano for being overprotective. The man had good reason to be. He shouldn't trust anyone. He had way too many enemies to take chances. In fact, his own wife had been murdered in a boating "accident" fifteen years ago.

Romano knew it hadn't been an accident. It had been an explosion so strong that it had taken days to identify the scattered remains of Romano's wife's body. The hit had been premeditated and flawlessly executed.

From what Damon had learned from the staff who had been in his home for decades, Romano had been crushed. He'd loved Elena dearly. Soon after the murder of his wife, he'd tightened the reins on his daughter, eventually deciding to keep her sequestered at the compound at all times.

At least Gemma had a hobby. Not just any hobby. When she played the piano, the entire vibe in the compound improved. She was playing now as Damon made his way to the exit. Today's music was modern and rather angry, which made him smirk. Everyone in the household could judge her mood by her music.

The hairs on the back of Damon's neck stood on end as he left the compound to retrieve the video, and he felt uneasy the entire time he was gone. For good reason.

When Damon pulled up outside the gate to the compound, he knew immediately that something was off. Very off. First of all, no one was at the gate to open it. Usually, there were at least two men standing guard and two others patrolling nearby.

Moments later, an explosion tore through the entire compound with enough force to shake Damon's SUV, rattle the windows, and knock his sunglasses off the dash. "*Fuck,*" he shouted into thin air as he pulled out his personal cell and dialed the number he would only use in an extreme emergency.

He didn't need to wait for anyone to answer. He only needed to place the code blue call and hang up. Reinforcements would arrive soon. But it would be too late. It was clearly already too late.

After parking the SUV on the side of the road, Damon tucked a gun in the back of his pants, made sure his knife was secured to his leg, and hopped out of the car carrying a third weapon in his palm. From the sound of things, he'd be a fool to enter the compound unarmed.

He scaled the high fencing that should have kept anyone out. He knew where and how to enter though, and he did so without issue. He did not rush toward the mansion. It was taking on heavy gunfire, and smoke was billowing up from somewhere in the center—most likely a result of the explosion.

"Fuck," Damon muttered under his breath several times. This hadn't been in the plan. This was not the FBI. Someone else had gotten to Romano before Damon could finish and get him taken down legally. It pissed him the fuck off. An entire year of research and investigation up in smoke.

Romano had pissed off so many people in the last several decades there was no telling who'd decided to take him down a notch—or perhaps take him out of the game entirely. Probably someone challenging him for his territory.

With absolutely no backup and no way to know who the fuck was invading, all Damon could do was remain hidden in the tree line and watch.

The job was quick. Not surprising. Less than ten minutes later, two armored vehicles came around from the other side of the house, broke through the front gates without pausing, and sped off.

A year of work down the drain in a heartbeat. Before the police arrived, Damon scoured the entire compound as fast as possible.

He tore the place up in search of Gemma, fearing the worst. His heart raced every time he entered another room, expecting to find her body in her suite or the kitchen or the theatre. That didn't happen, though. What happened was much worse. There was no sign of her anywhere.

It was obvious she'd been taken because everyone else who'd been in the compound when Damon had left earlier was now dead. Her father and everyone on his staff. They'd been shot or stabbed and left to bleed out in every room. Damon didn't find a single person with a pulse.

When he found the location of the initial explosion, he cursed. It most likely hadn't killed anyone. It had simply created chaos and provided an entrance to the property.

The compound was destroyed. Small fires burned in nearly every room. Walls had been destroyed by smaller explosives. What was left was a strange eerie silence.

Damon was done there. There wasn't a damn thing he could do about the bodies, and he wasn't going to find Gemma today. He had to get out of dodge before anyone showed up. So much for prosecuting the bad guys the legal way. Someone else had done it for them and saved the taxpayers a lot of money. The question was, who the fuck had raided Salinardi Romano's inner sanctum, and what had they done with Gemma?

Damon suspected the worse and vowed to dedicate his life to finding Gemma no matter how long it took.

CHAPTER TWO

Present day…

"Are you insane?" Robert Suthers asked as he leaned back in his desk chair, eyeing Damon suspiciously.

Damon shrugged as he met his friend's gaze. "Perhaps, but I'm still going to do it."

Robert lurched forward, setting his elbows on his desk across from Damon. The two of them were sitting in his fancy office in his exclusive club, Roses and Thorns. "That is the craziest, most hair-brained idea you've ever had, and I've known you for most of your life. You've done some batshit things in that time, but this one takes the cake, man. I think you need someone to jump in with a moral compass and tell you no. So, *no*. Don't do it. If your father were alive…"

Damon narrowed his gaze. "Don't bring my father into this. He lived barely above the law, and you know it."

Robert was ten years older than Damon, so they hadn't known each other when they were young, but their fathers had been friends, and both men had died within a week of each other. Damon's father from a "heart attack." Robert's father from a "stroke."

If it had just been one of them, it might not have raised suspicions, but Damon and Robert knew there was a good chance neither death had been a coincidence.

Damon had been twenty-five at the time. He'd recently gotten his master's in finance and moved back to the Denver area. After the dust had settled, he'd reconnected with Robert and subsequently joined his club, Roses and Thorns.

Even though Damon's mother had raised him largely on her own, he'd had visitation with his father, and he'd turned into the same kind of Dominant man his father had been. Unlike his father, Damon preferred to practice safe, sane, consensual dominance, and he did so at Roses and Thorns.

Damon drew in a deep breath, tapping his fingertips along the arms of the expensive leather chair he occupied. He refused to let Robert ruffle his feathers. He'd already made up his mind. In fact, the deed was done. He'd made the wire transfer this morning. Even though he hadn't picked up the package yet, he was already a slave owner.

Robert groaned and rolled his head in both directions. "Jesus," he muttered, "you've already put this plan in motion, haven't you?"

"Yes. I'm not asking for your permission, nor am I interested in your opinions. I'm only telling you about it so that if things go south and I disappear from the planet, at least one person will have known where I went."

Robert narrowed his gaze. "Fuck."

Damon didn't let himself flinch. He'd expected Robert to react this way. He couldn't blame him.

"You've got more money than you have brains."

Damon smirked. "Probably. Might as well put it to good use."

"How about a nice charity? You could donate it to an antihuman-trafficking organization and save hundreds of women instead of just one," Robert suggested.

"I could, but then I'd spend my entire life wondering and worrying about Gemma."

Robert sighed. "Somehow, I knew this day would come."

"Then why are you so shocked?" Damon asked.

"Because it's fucking dangerous, and I'd hoped you would have forgotten Gemma and moved on with your life."

It was Damon's turn to lean forward, closing the distance between himself and his friend. "I've never once forgotten her, not even for a day. Not a single day. I lie awake at night worrying about her. I fucking let her down. Now, I'm going to get her back."

"How long have you been planning this?"

"Over a year," Damon admitted.

"Fuck. How long has it been since you last saw her?"

"Three years." Damon winced. Three mother-fucking long years that he'd spent trying to find her under the radar. Until two weeks ago, he hadn't had a single lead on her possible whereabouts. Finally, he'd gotten his first tip, and he'd been crawling the walls ever since.

"You're toying with the Italian mob. If they get a single inkling that you're fucking with them, they'll have you killed and make you disappear from this earth as if you never existed," Robert reminded Damon.

"I'm well aware, and I'm not fucking with them. If they figure out who I am, so what? They can dig around in my past all they want. They won't find a single reason not to trust me. As far as they'll be concerned, I'm just another rich bastard who's willing to pay top dollar for a well-trained slave. I'm sure I'm not the only buyer with connections to the Italian mob who bid on a woman and won the auction."

Robert picked up a pen and flicked it back and forth over the desk, staring at Damon before sighing heavily. "Fuck." He drew in a breath. "You've spent ten years trying to nail this bastard. Now you're going to walk right into his den? You don't even know who he is."

Damon nodded. "Right now, I don't even care. Right now, I only care about one woman, and I'm going to fucking rescue her if I die doing so."

Robert sighed. "Does Jagger know about this?"

Damon shook his head. "No. I'm not going to tell him until after the purchase."

Robert groaned. "This is fucking dangerous. You should tell him. He's going to be pissed."

Damon shrugged. "He's going to have to be pissed. If I alert the FBI, they'll show up at the meeting location. The risk of losing Gemma is too high. I won't risk her life."

"Jesus. What's the plan?"

"You sure you want to know? It's not pretty."

Robert narrowed his gaze. "Just tell me the fucking plan, Damon."

"The plan is to attend this private party, pick up Gemma, and get her the fuck out of there." It wasn't complicated. Not when he put it like that.

"When?"

"Friday night. Apparently, the seller likes to make a spectacle out of his sales." Damon winced at the thought of dragging his purchase out for the entire evening, but it couldn't be helped. He wished he could have simply wired the money, picked up the woman, and gotten out of dodge.

On the flip side, doing so wouldn't have put him any closer to nailing the bastards to the wall. This circus show would give Damon the opportunity to collect information. He needed to remind himself of that detail and focus his attention on the attendees and discovering who the seller was.

Fat chance of him managing to gather many details, though. He'd never expected to find himself in this situation.

A scenario where he fucking cared about the woman he was trying to rescue. His life's ambition still existed, but for the last three years, it had been on the back burner while he'd worked his ass off trying to find Gemma.

Finally, he'd gotten lucky. His eyes were strained from digging around on the dark web for hours every day, searching for anything that would lead him to Gemma. He'd nearly pissed himself when he'd finally stumbled upon her two weeks ago. After three years.

He hadn't seen her face. It had been blurred by the seller, but there was no mistaking her body. It was her. Bile rose in his throat even now at the memory burned in his mind for all time. Sweet, funny, innocent Gemma's naked body plastered on the web for auction.

The mole on her left shoulder had been his first clue. That's what he'd been looking for. He should be glad she hadn't looked altered in any way. Her tits were still high and firm. Granted, he'd never seen her nipples before, but he had now. Rosy disks with hard points.

Damon closed his eyes and squeezed them shut as he visualized her pussy. He definitely hadn't been acquainted with that until two weeks ago. Pink folds. Presumably untouched. After all, that's what the seller was auctioning off —a well-trained, virginal slave.

"She's not going to be anything like the woman you knew after three years in captivity," Robert pointed out. "She's going to be fucked up, possibly permanently."

"I'm well aware. I'll take care of her. Get her the help she needs."

Robert groaned. "You're half in love with her, and it's probably misplaced. She's an illusion. You don't know what she's really like. You planning to become her new Master? Move her from one captivity to another? Force her to love you back?"

Damon slammed his hands on the desk. "Don't you fucking act like I'm some kind of animal. You know me better than that."

"Do I? Damon, I would've said so an hour ago before you strutted into my office and laid this plan of yours out in front of me. Now, I'm seriously wondering if you've thought this through. A million dollars is a lot of money to pay for a woman. I'm worried you're hoping to stroll into the sunset with her, and that's incredibly unlikely."

"You think I don't know that?"

Robert lifted a brow.

Damon growled. "I've looked at this from every angle. I know she's going to be fucked up. I understand that my goal needs to be rescuing her. That's it. After I get her the fuck out of there, then I'll figure out what's best for her. Don't fucking insinuate otherwise."

Robert took a deep breath and let it out slowly. "You never told me much about that undercover job working for her father, Damon, but I suspect it was fucking ugly."

Damon interrupted him. "The only reason I let you know I was working that job was because I was gone for almost a year, and you would've sent an army to find me."

Robert chuckled. "That's true."

"And, if you'll recall, I never did tell you where I'd been. You figured it out on your own."

"It wasn't hard since you resurfaced looking like someone I'd never met two days after Salinardi Romano's complex was raided, leaving him and everyone who worked for him dead and his daughter missing."

Damon rubbed his forehead. That about summed it up.

Robert cleared his throat and spoke in a softer voice. "It wasn't the first time you went undercover and disappeared for months at a time, Damon. I'm well aware of your save-the-universe complex, though I'm sure few other people are. I would never whisper a word of what I know to a single soul, and you know that."

Damon gave a sharp nod. He did. He wouldn't be sitting here in his friend's office informing him of his plans for next weekend if he didn't trust him implicitly.

"That being said," Robert continued, "I'm worried about you. The most you ever told me was that there was a woman who'd been kidnapped from the estate and never found. I suspected you had feelings for her at the time, but I had no idea you'd spent the last three years plotting to rescue her."

Damon wished it were that altruistic. He wished he could look his friend in the eye and tell him that all he cared about was saving Gemma from a madman so she could resume her regularly scheduled life.

However, none of that had ever been true. Damon wanted Gemma. He had then, and the feeling had never left him. He would acknowledge that the chances of him finding a woman who was intact enough to live a normal life were slim, but he had to try.

"Please don't get yourself killed. No one is worth it. You're too valuable to the human race to risk your life for a woman who's probably broken beyond repair."

Robert had schooled his voice to be as kind as possible, but part of Damon wanted to reach across the desk and grab his friend by the shirt.

It wasn't rational, of course. Robert was right. Still, Damon had to try, for her.

For himself.

CHAPTER THREE

Damon's brow was furrowed as he stepped out of his SUV
and handed the keys to the valet. It didn't matter. No one
could see his expression behind the elaborate mask he wore.
He'd pulled over five minutes ago to put the mask on before
arriving at the address he'd been sent to in the warehouse
district.

If he were an average, everyday human, he would be
shitting himself right now, but he wasn't. He had Italian blood
running through him, and he suspected several of the people
he would encounter tonight were cut from the same cloth.

Damon had paid a cool million for Gemma. Every man
who was purchasing a slave tonight had undoubtedly paid a
similar price. A million dollars seemed to be the going rate for
a well-trained, virginal slave girl.

Damon gritted his teeth. He'd clenched his jaws so many
times in the last few days that they ached.

The young man who sped off in Damon's vehicle had been
wearing a ski mask. It would appear that the seller intended to
protect the identities of his employees as well as the buyers.

The fanfare was over the top. Damon would have much

rather paid his fee and picked up his purchase, but that wasn't part of the deal. This was an elaborate game cooked up by some sick fuck who enjoyed seriously fucked-up debauchery.

Damon hoped by the end of the night he'd have at least an inkling as to who'd made these arrangements and who'd attended, but he had his doubts.

Apparently, each participant had been assigned a specific arrival time. No sooner. No later. This prevented any two people from arriving at the same time and risk exposing their identity.

To further protect themselves, they'd been encouraged to rent their vehicles so that no license plates could be traced back to any individual without some difficulty.

Damon was under no illusion that whoever the ringleader was, he had access to all the cars and was probably scanning the information with each arrival. Total anonymity was an illusion. It always was.

Damon took the few paces toward the warehouse door. It was unassuming. It didn't look remotely important. As he reached for the handle, it opened from the inside, and another masked man stepped back, waving his hand in a gesture indicating Damon should enter.

Rule number seven thousand: speak as little as possible to avoid being recognized by voice. At least Damon wouldn't be making polite conversation with anyone.

Damon handed the doorman the name of the slave he'd purchased handwritten on a piece of paper. *Marigold.* The man in turn grabbed an envelope from the table behind him and handed it to Damon, who stuck it in the pocket inside his suit jacket. This was his ticket. The receipt that indicated he was the owner of slave Marigold.

The doorman then motioned for Damon to hold his arms out at his sides and spread his legs. The man patted him up and down. Damon had left his cell phone and all weapons in the car as instructed.

A glance at the table indicated there were two envelopes left, which meant three men had arrived before Damon, having been assigned earlier arrival times.

When the masked doorman was done with his pat down, he pointed toward another door down a hallway, and Damon headed in that direction, straightening his suit jacket as he walked. The dress code had been among the rules. Three-piece suits. Black. White shirts. Black dress shoes and socks.

The mask and information had been mailed to Damon at a P.O. box he'd been assigned, and he'd picked the items up yesterday. He felt a bit like he was about to perform on the set of *Beauty and the Beast*, except that would be true of every guest at this bizarre gathering.

After opening the door at the end of the hall, he stepped into a dim corridor and followed it for several yards until he emerged into a large open space.

This was it. This was where the exchange would occur. A dozen or so men were already in attendance, each seated in their assigned chair. The chairs were spread out, several feet between each one in every direction.

As one of the auction winners, Damon headed for seat number three in the front row and fought his nerves as he lowered his body onto the chair. He'd done his best to glance around at the guests who'd arrived before him, but there was no fucking way in hell to ascertain who any of them might be.

No one spoke a word.

There was no stage, but the chairs were arranged in a way that made it clear there was to be a show in front of him. The six buyers were in front, their chairs wide apart at a slight curve. The next row of seats was behind those and in between. The next row was arranged similarly so that everyone could easily see the staging area without difficulty.

There were approximately two dozen seats, give or take. He wondered what it cost to simply be a witness to this event —someone who had failed to bid high enough for the pleasure of owning a slave. The losers were given first dibs for the chance to be a voyeur. Perhaps at the next ceremony, they would be able to afford the high price of owning their own slave.

Jesus.

Damon took a deep breath, trying not to move around much or appear as rattled as he was. Who the fuck were all these men? What a goddamn shitshow.

He'd expected six buyers because he'd chosen from six slaves. Marigold, Oleander, Jasmine, Tulip, Daffodil, and Lily. The madman who'd kidnapped these women and turned them into property had named them all after poisonous flowers.

Sweat gathered on Damon's brow, not because it was particularly hot in here but because he was fighting back the bile rising in his throat. He'd purchased a human being, and he was here to collect his slave. Who did that?

If this place were raided tonight, Damon would undoubtedly be sent to prison. It wasn't likely that Jagger or Robert would have the clout to vouch for him and get him out of this mess.

Another forty-five minutes passed before it appeared everyone had arrived. Damon paid close attention to the man who stood in the shadows along the edge of the staging area, holding a microphone.

He was a large man—tall and overweight—but so were half the fucking people living in Denver, so there was no way to readily identify him by his build. In addition, as soon as he spoke, it was clear he was using a voice-altering device to protect his identity.

This guy ran a tight ship. Damon had to give him credit.

"Gentleman…" He cleared his throat and continued, "Thank you for joining us tonight. It's my great pleasure to present tonight's slaves to their new owners. I deal only in the finest products in my line of business and personally guarantee that each of the girls in my possession is and remains a virgin. Untouched. Each girl is trained to be the obedient slave I advertise."

Damon held his beath. *Holy mother of God.* This was bad.

"My flowers are not put up for auction until they demonstrate they are ready to behave in the manner expected of them. For tonight's six slaves, that day has come."

Damon pursed his lips. Gemma had been here three years. Had this asshole kept her because he'd wanted enough time to pass that few people would remember who she was? Or was Gemma feisty enough that she hadn't bent to his will as quickly as others?

The Gemma he'd known easily could have given this fucker a run for his money, but how broken was she now?

"In a moment, the slaves will be led out and instructed to present themselves. I will give them orders. They will obey without hesitation. They will be blindfolded and remain that way throughout the presentation ceremony. I would advise their new owners to keep them blindfolded until they have been transported to their new dwellings to avoid any possibility that they might figure out where they're located."

There was some fidgeting on both sides of Damon and behind him. He wasn't the only person in the room who was either uncomfortable or nervous. There could be any number of reasons. Half of these guys probably had a hard-on from the anticipation.

"Without further ado, let's begin the demonstration. Trainers, please bring the slaves out."

Damon sucked in a breath and blinked a few times as six men dressed all in black with ski masks led six naked women onto the staging area. The women wore only two items: a white blindfold that securely covered their eyes and a white collar. They were led onto the stage by leashes.

Damon instantly recognized Gemma, and his heart seized. He deduced that the women were led out in the particular order of their buyer because she was positioned in front of him, only a few yards separating them.

Damon wanted to jump up from his seat, grab her, and get the fuck out of this godforsaken warehouse, but he didn't dare move. He had no choice but to see this night through or risk everything. He reminded himself that whatever happened in the next few hours was undoubtedly nothing compared to what she'd been through in the past three years.

Hold on for me, baby. Just a bit longer.

Damon stared at her. He could see no evidence she'd been mistreated. Not physically, at least. That was indeed what the seller had advertised. No permanent scarring. No piercings. The slaves would be delivered unharmed, with the exception of a small discreet tattoo that indicated their ownership.

Damon had yet to see where the tattoo might be located, which made his mouth go dry as the trainer guided Gemma to spin in a circle several times before stopping her so that she faced the crowd.

Like all the slaves, she had her forearms crossed at the small of her back, her hands wrapped around each wrist. Her shoulders were pulled back, forcing her tits high.

Her hair was longer than the last time he'd seen her, down to her butt. It didn't appear to have been cut in three years. Her skin was the same golden brown. Her pussy was shaved bare. Or had she been waxed? He'd read something about that in the contract, but he hadn't dwelled long on the details because he hadn't been able to without feeling nauseous. Besides, he hadn't cared. He simply wanted her back.

Back? What a joke. He'd never had her in the first place.

He couldn't be sure she would even remember who he was. It was possible she wouldn't have a single clue.

No. He refused to believe that. It wasn't likely. She would know him. She had to. Perhaps it was wishful thinking, but he'd harbored the idea that she'd secretly liked him going back four years ago.

How did he know? Because she'd paid no attention to him. She'd gone out of her way to ignore him and avoid him. It had taken him a while to figure out why. He'd chuckled to himself one day when she'd stormed into her father's office and started yelling at him about some employee he'd fired.

Rafael. Or perhaps Ricardo. It didn't matter. Gemma had paced before her father, accusing him of ruining her life.

Her father had calmly explained that his staff was under strict instructions to keep their eyes and, more importantly, their hands to themselves. If any of his employees so much as glanced at her, they would be fired on the spot.

Damon couldn't imagine how lonely that would have been for a teenager who couldn't leave her home and wasn't permitted to speak to any of the male staff. Damon may have invented his belief in his mind, but he took her total avoidance of him to mean she liked him and didn't want him to get fired.

The booming sound of the announcer dragged Damon back to the present. Not that he'd removed his gaze from Gemma, but he was yanked back into the present. "Slaves, wait."

At the command, Gemma spread her legs shoulder-width apart. She kept her head high, chin raised.

It was stifling in this room. Damon hoped he could remain calm.

"Slaves, inspection."

Gemma kept her feet spread wide but released her hands

to lift them up and clasp them behind her head, pulling her elbows back, breasts thrust forward. It was lewd. Obscene.

The crazy thing was that Damon knew these positions. He'd seen them performed many times at Roses and Thorns. The strict protocol for slaves was practiced by many people in the community.

However, the members of Roses and Thorns were consenting adults. They signed wavers. They chose to submit of their own free will. This display of forced slavery was vile and disgusting and difficult to witness.

The trainers kept a hand on the leashes at all times, giving a slight tug as if the women needed the reminder to switch positions as the announcer went through a series of commands.

When the slaves were commanded to assume the Nadu position, they each lowered to their knees, spread their legs wide, and dropped their butts onto their heels. Backs straight, shoulders back. Chins up. Hands resting on their thighs, palms up.

This was when Damon realized where they'd been marked. On their inner thighs. He couldn't see the tattoos, but they were there. Distinctive small markings high on their inner thighs. *Jesus.* That must have hurt like a motherfucker.

The trainers circled their charges, tapping them in various places to encourage them to lift their chins higher, spread their knees wider, or pull their shoulders back farther.

Gemma was fucking gorgeous, and in another world under different circumstances, Damon would have loved for her to present herself to him like this. He'd never been particularly interested in a Master/slave arrangement, but if he'd found a submissive who craved deep protocol, he would have ensured her needs were met.

Could Gemma have craved this sort of life if she'd been given the choice? He would never know. Her autonomy had been taken. Stripped. Stomped on. Destroyed. He had no idea what her mental state might be like and if she could recover from this brainwashing.

"Turn. Face away from your new Masters. Show them your assets. Humble."

Damon swallowed over the lump in his throat. Everyone in this room was watching his woman as she gracefully rocked forward onto her hands, crawled in a half circle, and lowered her torso to the floor. She reached as far forward as she could with her palms on the concrete, her forehead pressed to the floor between her elbows.

Damon let his eyes close for a moment, trying to settle his nerves as she tucked her knees up under her, spread them wide, and lowered her butt between her feet. He could see everything. Everyone in the room could, too. The tight pucker of her ass and the pink folds of her pussy. Her full breasts were pressed to the concrete, the pebbled points of her nipples scraping the floor.

He was going to pass out if he didn't breathe. He was going to cause a scene if he did.

"Slaves, crawl to your Master and show him what you can do with your mouth."

Damon stiffened as the trainer tugged on Gemma's leash to encourage her to rise and then led her across the floor in Damon's direction.

He blinked several times as she got closer. Fuck, she was beautiful. But dammit, this could not be happening.

When she was close enough to bump into Damon's legs, he swallowed hard. His cock was stiff between his legs, which pissed him off. It was impossible not to be affected by her even though the circumstances were otherworldly.

With another tug on her leash, Gemma leaned back on her knees and set her hands on Damon's shins. She ran them up and down his legs from his ankles to his knees in a sensuous display of total obedience. The only sign that all was not right with the universe was the fact that her hands were shaking and her lips were pursed.

Damon didn't move a muscle, except his growing cock. He took small shallow breaths, trying to remain focused and block out the fact that two dozen people were watching, and it was clear by the context clues that Gemma was expected to give him a blow job.

She pushed his legs apart, gently, and then inched closer on her knees.

The trainer tapped her thigh, and she flinched before parting her knees wider.

Damon wanted to yank the leash out of the man's hand and swat the fucking crop away at the same time. He had no business touching Gemma.

Gemma's hands slid to Damon's thighs, and she began a sensual dance, tormenting him with her perfect body and the feel of her palms on his tight muscles.

If it weren't for her shaking hands, Damon would never believe this wasn't consensual. He didn't glance either direction to see what else was happening around him. He couldn't take his gaze off Gemma, nor did he want to.

The trainer suddenly lifted his crop and gave Gemma a quick swat to her left nipple.

She gasped as her body flinched, shifting her hands to Damon's belt a moment later.

Damon was seeing red. The fucking guy was lucky he was alive. Damon didn't know how the hell he was going to remain calm and get this farce of a presentation over with, but somehow, he had to find the will.

Gemma deftly unfastened his belt before going to work on the button and then the zipper of his suit pants. She tugged his shirttail out next and unbuttoned the lower three buttons on it to spread it out to the sides.

When her palms came to his cock, he moaned involuntarily. He wasn't alone. Other noises filled the air.

The announcer reminded him that he was about to get blown in front of an audience with his next words. He chuckled first. "Don't worry. These slaves have never sucked another man's cock before. You will be their first. However, they have spent hours training for this moment, practicing the sensual art of sucking a man off with mannequins and rubber cocks. Months of training has prepared them to not only deep throat but swallow. You won't be disappointed."

Damon's vision blurred. The man's words were horrific, but it was difficult to focus with Gemma's fingers roaming all over his hard-on before easing his underwear down and wrapping her palm around his shaft.

Fuck. She was good at this. He was going to blow and make a fool of himself at any moment. If he'd known he would be expected to orgasm in front of all these people, he would have rubbed one off an hour ago.

With practiced skill, Gemma teased the length of his cock for several seconds before dragging her finger through the slit in the tip and bringing it to her mouth.

She tipped her head back so he could watch her and moaned as she sucked his pre-come from her finger.

Damon's breath hitched. *Jesus. Fucking hell.*

She was so fucking gorgeous, and this entire scenario was so fucked up and wrong.

He didn't have a chance to fully process what he was witnessing before she lowered her face to his cock and flicked her tongue over the tip.

Damon flinched. *Fuck. Fuck me. Fuck.* He didn't want to be so damn aroused with her like this, but he couldn't stop it. He wanted to touch her, but he didn't dare. It felt wrong. He instead gripped the edges of his chair at his outer thighs.

Without hesitation, Gemma lowered her face all the way down, swallowing his entire cock into the back of her throat.

Damon's eyes rolled back. He'd received plenty of blowjobs in his life, but not a single one compared to this. No woman had ever sucked him in this deep. Few women could do so or come anywhere close. They usually wrapped their palm around the base and mimicked their mouth with their hands.

How was she not choking?

Suddenly, she stiffened, not moving. She took a deep breath through her nose and held it. She did it again.

Damon worried she was struggling to breathe. He considered interfering, especially when her teeth scraped his dick.

The trainer grabbed a fistful of her hair and gave a sharp tug.

Gemma whimpered as she released Damon's cock, replacing her mouth with her hands. She was panting.

The trainer gave another tug, forcing her head back so her neck was elongated and her head was arched too far. She gasped. "I'm sorry, Sir," she whispered. "I'll get it right, Sir."

When the trainer continued to hold her head back as if he was shocked by her insolence, Damon finally intervened. He reached forward, captured the man's wrist, and growled in a low voice, "Release her."

That was it. Two low words. It was enough.

The trainer let go of her head and took a slight step back. Thank God.

Damon cupped the back of her head, rubbing it gently, hoping his actions would speak louder than the words he was about to utter. He didn't want the seller to notice her slip up. There was no telling what would happen if she didn't follow every detail of protocol.

She was his now. Fuck this goddamn demonstration. He'd

paid for her. By all rights, she was his, and no one was going to fucking touch her.

He took a deep breath, leaned in, and took a risk, murmuring to her low and directly, hoping she could hear him without anyone else noticing. The trainer wouldn't miss his words, however, so they were calculated. "Finish your task, slave."

She sucked in a breath. Her lips parted. She didn't move for a few long seconds.

Damon feared she wouldn't do as she was told. He couldn't blame her, but he also didn't want any more attention brought to her. Or to him.

With his hand still on the back of her head, threaded in her hair, he gently urged her forward.

As if snapping out of her strange state of shock, she quickly lowered her face back to his cock. As she fumbled blindly, trying to hit her mark, Damon gripped the base and guided it to her lips.

Her hair fell around her face in a curtain, blocking anyone from seeing what she was doing, and giving Damon the perfect opportunity to slide his hand up onto his shaft, preventing her from being able to take more than a few inches of him.

There was no way he could stop this from happening. He was going to come. She was going to have to swallow. But he didn't need to fucking choke her or traumatize her any more than she already was.

She was indeed well-trained. Her mouth was heaven on his cock. She hesitated only one more time—when her lips bumped into his fingers, surprising her as she realized his intention.

He buried his fingers in her hair and stroked her scalp with his fingertips. No one could see that tenderness because her hair was so thick it covered his actions.

Damon stared down at her, blocking out the world, blocking out everything. He had to focus his attention on the precious woman between his legs and pretend she didn't mind sucking him off, anything to speed the process along so she wouldn't have to suck him one second longer than necessary.

The feel of her hair between his fingers, her lips around his erection, her hands on his thighs. *Focus.* He sucked in a breath and closed his eyes as he succumbed, somehow managing to give her a warning squeeze against her neck.

Gemma pulled him as deep as she could with his hand in the way, hollowed her cheeks, and swallowed every drop as he pulsed into her throat.

Fuck. Jesus. He was shaking worse than her as he pulled himself back together.

"Thank you, Master," she murmured, shaking him out of his state of bliss.

CHAPTER FOUR

Damon clenched his jaw as he stared down at her while he tucked his cock back into his pants, followed by his shirt before zipping and buttoning. She was still pressed between his legs, but she'd settled back on her heels once more, knees parted wide, hands on her thighs, palms up, head bowed this time.

He was still holding her, his hand having slipped to her neck. He gave a squeeze, reassuring her the only way he could before releasing her to avoid drawing attention to himself.

She seemed slightly more relaxed than before. Maybe he was reading her wrong, but he hoped he'd done something to ease her stress.

Damon focused all his attention on the woman in front of him, ignoring the noises around him. No one was speaking, but there were a lot of sounds. Mostly moaning and grunting.

Gemma never broke her pose. She seemed to relax further with each passing moment, focusing on her breathing. Perhaps she'd found coping mechanisms and had used them to survive the past three years. He wanted to get the fuck out of here and prayed this charade was over.

Had these women done enough to prove their worth? Had they put on enough of a show for the paying customers who came to watch the spectacle?

"Rise, slaves," the announcer finally commanded.

Watching Gemma rise to her feet was both beautiful and annoying. The fact that she'd been forced to perfect these moves against her will infuriated Damon. He couldn't take much more of this. It needed to end. He was seconds from ending it himself.

She stood before him, her hands clasped behind her back once again, feet spread, shoulders squared. Damn, she was lovely. He vowed that no one but him would ever see her naked body again after this night.

And who the fuck did he think he was? He needed to screw his head on tight. She had no reason to share her body with *him* either. The moment they left here, he would return her autonomy.

"Masters, please take some time to examine the merchandise. Reassure yourselves that you're getting what you've paid for. I ask that you not penetrate the slaves until you've left the warehouse, but if you'd like to ensure she's untouched, you're welcome to do so. We'll bring out an exam table and set it up in the middle of the room."

Gemma's jaw tightened as she winced. It was subtle. Hopefully, no one noticed.

Damon was aware of the other Masters rising to their feet, and he did so too, praying he could get out of here. They each began to circle their slave.

Damon stepped close to her, aware of her trembling as he set his hands on her biceps and stroked them up to her shoulders. He tipped her head back as if he were examining her features or her mouth and nose.

He leaned over to whisper in her ear. "Relax. We're done here. No one is going to examine you."

She swallowed but gave no other indication she'd heard him. Except a moment later, her shoulders relaxed, the stiffness in her body easing.

Damon hated all these people gawking at her, but he was kind of glad she had been blindfolded the entire time and unable to see them. Hopefully, she'd gone into her head and pretended no one else was in the room.

"I'd like to thank everyone for coming tonight. When you're satisfied with your purchases, you may lead your slave back out the way you entered. Again, I highly recommend you leave her blindfold in place until you've reached your destinations. She is your property now to do with as you please, but slaves adapt better when they are uncertain of their location."

What a fucked-up asshole. Damon wished he knew who the fuck was holding the microphone so he could have him arrested in the middle of the night. As it was, he didn't know a goddamn thing about anyone in this room.

The most he could do would be to send the FBI to this location tomorrow morning and hope they found some trace of evidence about what had gone down here tonight, but he knew the place would be wiped clean. Not a single speck of dust would be out of place.

Damon had considered calling his handler before he came tonight. He'd thought about it several times. He could have at least called Jagger and forced himself to get his friend's outside perspective, but in the end, Damon hadn't wanted to take the risk that anything might cause Gemma to slip through his fingers.

Perhaps he was being selfish and should have considered the good of all six slaves who'd been sold here tonight, and he'd seriously dug deep while making this decision.

In the end, he'd decided to save one woman. His woman. Gemma. He would do everything in his power to rescue the others and every past and future victim of human trafficking, but tonight, he could only focus on Gemma.

If he'd told the FBI where the ceremony would be taking place, they might have done something to tip off the seller, and Gemma could have been gone to Damon forever. It was a risk he hadn't been willing to take.

He didn't work for the FBI. He'd never taken a dime from them. He was an informant. Nothing else. He provided information when he thought it would be helpful, period. Except this time. This time, he'd withheld it. He would share. But not today. Not yesterday.

Gemma was shaking. He needed to get her the fuck out before someone noticed.

The trainer handed Damon her leash as if he were passing off a piece of property to its new and rightful owner. A dog or a goat. Not a human.

Damon took the leash but didn't apply any pressure to it. Instead, he settled his hand on Gemma's neck and guided her toward the back of the room and the hallway where he'd entered the staging area. He wanted to be one of the first to leave this living hell. A line would form as everyone waited for their cars. He didn't want to be standing in it with a trembling Gemma at his side.

Several people rose from their seats, gawking at Gemma's body as he passed them. No one touched her. That was a good thing. He might have decked anyone who dared to reach out a hand.

There were no words spoken either. Blessedly. Maybe she wouldn't realize how many men had watched her perform.

Only two people were ahead of Damon, forming a line. The cars would be brought to the entrance one at a time, and the next person would have to wait for the man ahead of them to drive away before the next vehicle would pull up.

Damon was also grateful that no one got too close to him.

He left several feet between him and the man in front of him. The person behind him did the same.

Gemma was shaking harder. He feared she might faint. He wanted to lift her into his arms. He wanted to take his jacket off and cover her body. He did neither.

Damon would not risk drawing attention to them. He would cause heads to turn if he appeared soft. He was supposed to be a ruthless slave owner. That was his role until he got out of here. As soon as he had her in the car, all bets were off.

He set a hand on her waist and gave a squeeze, surrounding her as much as he could from behind, his lips coming to her ear again. "Hold on for me, baby. Another few minutes."

She shivered as if she weren't sure she could trust him. And how could she? She had no idea who'd just bought her. She had to be scared out of her mind.

The first man left, and the second stepped forward.

"We're almost there," he reassured her.

She didn't respond. Her hands were clasped at her back, and when he set his palm over them, he realized she was tense. Her nails were probably digging into her skin.

Damon kept his other hand on her hip, the fucking leash looped over one finger, loosely. If he tugged it, she would probably freak out.

In the past decade, Damon had seen more leashed submissives than he could possibly count, and suddenly, the concept gave him a sour taste. He continually had to remind himself that the slaves he'd seen at Roses and Thorns were there voluntarily of their own free will. Robert didn't tolerate any behavior in his clubs that wasn't safe, sane, and consensual.

The man and woman in front of them left. Thank fuck. The masked man who'd been at the door when Damon entered was there now, too, blocking it. The sound of the car pulling away and Damon's pulling up was musical.

Finally, the man stepped aside and opened the door.

Damon guided Gemma out into the night air. She was naked. It was chilly. The valet opened the back door and held it so that Damon could help her into the back seat.

He was relieved when the guy took off jogging, presumably heading to retrieve the next vehicle.

The first thing Damon did after settling her on the seat was to unhook the leash from the front of her collar. He would take that damn collar off as soon as possible, but he didn't want to risk freaking her out by doing so now.

Next, Damon grabbed the seatbelt and reached across Gemma to buckle her in. He took a second to cup her face before shutting the door and hurrying to climb into the driver's seat. He couldn't get away from this fucking warehouse fast enough. He drove too fast, taking several turns so that he ended up between two other buildings where no one else would see him.

Putting the car in park, he shut off the engine, jumped out, and hurried to the backseat. No way could he drive all the way home and leave her sitting there fucking scared out of her mind.

He tugged his jacket off as quickly as possible, unbuckled her, and lifted her off the leather seat before climbing into her spot, shutting the door, and wrapping his jacket around her small body.

She stiffened against him. "Master?"

He cringed. He hadn't pulled off her blindfold yet, but he wanted to hold her for a moment and help her calm down before he added that detail.

She cleared her throat. "Damon?"

Damon froze. How the fuck did she know who he was? He eased the blindfold from her eyes, finally able to see them for the first time. What he saw broke his heart and made him glad she'd been blindfolded for the last two hours. Her eyes were empty. Hollow. Nothing.

After several seconds, she jerked her gaze downward. "Sorry, Master."

He flinched and lifted her chin. "Don't be sorry. Look at me, Gemma."

"But..." Her eyes were wild, and she blinked at him several times as if trying not to meet his gaze. She'd been trained not to look him in the eye. "My name is Marigold," she murmured.

His heart raced. *Please, God. She recognizes me. Surely, she can find herself in there, too.*

Ignoring her last statement to avoid confusing her, he spoke again. "How did you know it was me?"

"I..."

He urged her chin up again. "Please look at me."

She swallowed. "Your cologne," she whispered.

He smiled. "Good girl." He held her tighter. "You're safe now."

"Safe?" she asked the question as if it had no meaning to her.

"Yes. Safe."

"But... You bought me, Master."

He held her chin and narrowed his gaze at her. "Don't call me that. Call me Damon."

"But, Sir... Master..."

He shook his head. "I'm not your Master."

Her brow furrowed in confusion. "You paid for me."

"I did what was necessary to rescue you, Gemma. I don't own you."

She breathed heavier. Finally, tears fell down her cheeks.

Fuck. Jesus. What the hell was he going to do? He needed to get her out of here.

"We can't stay here, baby." He shouldn't call her that. He didn't own her. She wasn't his. She was a scared woman who'd been through fucking hell. But he couldn't stop the endearment from escaping his lips. It had happened more than once.

She said nothing. Her body was trembling violently. She was in shock.

Maybe he should call someone and ask them to come pick them up. Robert would do it. But that would take time, and he wanted to get the fuck out of here.

"Do you think you can be brave for me and curl up on the seat so I can drive?"

She said nothing.

Damon had a bag on the floor, and he yanked the zipper to open it, dragging out first a soft blanket and then a bottle of water. He tossed his jacket into the front passenger seat and wrapped the blanket around her trembling frame.

After twisting off the lid to the water, he tipped her head back and held it to her lips. "Drink for me, baby."

She stared at him, eyes blank again.

Fuck. "Drink," he commanded in a deeper voice. He hated resorting to ordering her, but he suspected it would work, and it did. She parted her lips and let him tip the water back. She even managed to swallow some of it, though most of it ran down her cheeks and soaked her hair.

It was something. He didn't want her dehydrated. He had protein bars and other snacks in the bag, but he doubted she was in any state to chew and swallow, nor did she appear to be malnourished. She'd eaten well enough for the past three years.

Damon kissed her forehead. "I'm going to lay you in this seat and pull the seatbelt over you to keep you safe, okay?"

She didn't respond. She was in shock or catatonic.

He needed to move. Sitting here wasn't helping things.

Maybe he should take her to a hospital or the fucking police station. He considered both fleetingly, but either option could possibly cause her to withdraw even more. Besides, she needed to make her own decisions. He would wait until she was capable of choosing and then let her decide.

When would that be? Tomorrow? The next day? *Fuck.*

Damon opened the door, gently lowered her on her side so that her back was against the seat, and pulled the seatbelt over her small frame.

Gemma panicked, eyes going wide, hands finding their way out of the cocoon of her blanket to bat at him.

Fuck it. He gave up on the seatbelt. He'd drive carefully. He bent over her, cupped her face, and kissed her forehead again. "You're safe, Gemma. Hold on for me. I'm going to get us out of here."

She gave no indication she'd heard him. Her eyes were squeezed closed as she curled into a tight ball, even ducking her head down under the covers.

Damon shut the door and got back in the front seat. His heart raced during the entire drive, and he said nothing. He didn't want to wake her or spook her further. He angled the rearview mirror down so he could glance at her every few seconds. She never moved.

CHAPTER FIVE

Finally, Damon pulled up to his estate and opened the gate. It seemed to take forever to open, and then he was through it and watching it close behind him before he drove the rest of the distance to circle behind his home. As soon as he was as close to the back of the house as he could get, he shut off the engine and jumped down from the SUV. A second later, he was yanking her door open.

He carefully set his hands on her. When she flinched, he said, "I'm going to carry you inside, baby." He didn't have a choice. He would have to manhandle her to get her into the house, and then... Well, he didn't know what the fuck was going to happen next. He'd have to wing it. One fucking second at a time.

No one was here. Margie, his housekeeper, typically came once a week, but he'd canceled her for the next few weeks. The gardener, too.

Damon had no fucking idea what to expect from Gemma, but he didn't want anyone else around to witness it.

He carried her limp body into the dark house, not turning

on any lights. He wasn't sure if he liked that she was practically non-responsive. He'd rather she scream or cry or something. The silence was worse.

Damon decided to go straight up the stairs and into the master suite. After his father had died, he'd considered moving into his estate, but he'd hated everything in it and everything it represented, so he'd sold it. This new home was far more his style, and it had nothing of his father.

Damon headed straight for his favorite armchair, turned on the soft lamp next to it, and sat. He cradled Gemma in his arms, but now what?

He had a million questions, starting with what she needed from him right now. Food? Water? A bath? Sleep?

He leaned her back in his arms, keeping her covered. "Gemma, baby, you're going to have to talk to me."

She flinched in his lap, her eyes flying open a second before her gaze shifted downward as if she'd just now realized where she was. "Master. I'm sorry." She squirmed in his lap, fighting him.

He considered letting her go, thinking she might feel confined by his grip on her. She needed agency over her body. Holding her wasn't accomplishing that.

The moment he loosened his hold, she slid to the floor and knelt before him, hands at her back, breasts thrust forward, the blanket slipping away.

Damon groaned inwardly. "No."

She flinched. "How may I serve you, Master."

He reached for her face and lifted it. "You will look me in the eye when you speak, Gemma," he demanded, realizing that was the only tone she'd responded to so far.

She looked lost and confused when she met his gaze. "Slaves don't look in their Master's eyes."

"Gemma. It's me. Damon. I'm not your Master. You're free."

She blinked. "You bought me. Why do you keep calling me Gemma?"

"I paid for you so you would be free, baby," he said softly. "You're not a slave. Your name is Gemma."

"I…" Her jaw hung open. She had no idea how to process this. "How do you know my old name?"

"Because I know you. You know me, too. Who am I?" he ordered.

"My Master."

"No. Gemma. Look at me. Who am I?"

She licked her lips. "Damon."

"That's right. You remember me."

She nodded slowly. "You worked for my father."

"Yes. I've spent the last three years looking for you, Gemma. Not to own you but to rescue you."

She shivered. "I'm a slave."

"You're not. Not anymore." He let that sit with her for a moment.

Tears fell down her face.

Thank fuck. The tears meant he was reaching her. It was fucking late, but they were on no timetable here. He'd stay up all night with her if that's what she needed.

"May I please hold you?" he asked softly.

She shuddered. She was still in the perfect slave position as if she didn't know how to behave otherwise. "Hold me?"

"Yes. On my lap." Maybe he was the world's largest asshole for touching her, but he needed to, and he suspected she also needed that kind of human contact.

"If that's what you wish, Master."

Fucking fuck. It seemed like she was wavering in and out of reality.

"Gemma, look at me," he ordered again.

She met his gaze, blinking. He couldn't be sure if she recognized him or not. It seemed to come and go. "Sir?"

He shook his head. "What's my name?"

"Damon," she whispered.

"That's the only thing you're permitted to call me. Understood?"

She blinked again. "But…"

"No buts. Damon. Nothing else."

"Master, I…"

My God. Damon's heart hurt.

She was a robot. He was going to have to retrain her to make her own decisions and recognize her autonomy. It was going to take time and a lot of fucking love. He could and would do it even if it took a decade—if it was what she wanted.

"Gemma," he said sternly to get her attention. She responded best when he commanded it. "My name," he insisted.

"Damon," she repeated.

"You're not a slave. Repeat that. I'm not a slave."

Her brow furrowed. "You bought me."

He shook his head. "Repeat my words, Gemma. I'm not a slave."

She swallowed. The command was completely out of her grasp.

"How were you disciplined when you misbehaved while you were being held, Gemma?"

Her mouth fell open, but no words came out. Either it was too painful, or there were too many responses. He didn't want to traumatize her further now, but he might need to discipline her to retrain her thinking.

He hated the idea, but if it worked… It might be the only way he could get her to respond.

"Did anyone spank you, Gemma?"

She shook her head. "No, Sir."

He groaned inwardly. He'd spent the last ten years looking for the perfect submissive who might submit to him and call him Sir. Now, he wanted to erase the word from the English language. Coming from Gemma after what she'd been through, it sounded vile and grated on his nerves.

He was surprised she had not been spanked, but then again, her owner hadn't wanted the slaves to be marked, so perhaps he hadn't used spanking as a form of punishment. He suspected her owner had used at the very least a crop to correct her behavior because the trainer had done so several times in front of Damon.

The man hadn't struck her hard. Just enough for her to feel the sting, a reminder. The fact that she hadn't been spanked might work in Damon's favor. He liked the idea of having a method of discipline that wouldn't bring forth any memories.

"Have you *ever* been spanked, Gemma?"

She gave him that blank stare again. "No, Sir."

Was he making the right decision here? It seemed insane to spank her. He'd just gotten her here. He wanted to erase all the bad. But for fuck's sake, he might need to call upon some out-of-the-box techniques in order to do so.

With every moment that passed, he had more questions. If no one had struck her body, how the fuck had they made her do as they said? He would find out, but he feared if she were capable of spilling all the details right now, he would end up picking up the lamp and throwing it across the room. That wouldn't help matters at all. The last thing he wanted was for Gemma to be afraid of him.

"I'm going to help you, Gemma. Help you find yourself. Help you climb out of the hell you've been living in and return to life."

She simply blinked.

"I don't own you. I know you can't grasp that, but it's true.

I am a Dominant. I enjoy the submission of others, Gemma, but only with their consent." He doubted he was making any sense, but he'd repeat himself every day until she understood.

She was trained to obey him. So, he'd have to use that to his advantage, twist it around, and force her to see things through a new lens. "I have rules," he stated, watching her closely.

"Of course. I will obey all of them, Master." This seemed to perk her up. *Jesus. Fuck.*

"Rule number one. You will not call me Master or Sir. You will address me as Damon. Understood?"

She slowly shook her head. The concept would not sink in.

"If you call me by any other moniker than Damon, I will spank you to remind you of the rule."

She flinched. "Yes, Sir." Her eyes went wide, and she gasped. "Master. Sir..." She started shaking. "I..."

"What's my name?"

Her lip trembled. She glanced down.

"Rule number two. You'll meet my gaze when you speak."

"I-I..." she stammered. He was confusing the fuck out of her, undoing everything she'd been taught. Could he, though? He needed professional help. But he wanted her consent for that, too.

"Stand, Gemma."

She rose with relative grace, but she was trembling and confused, so it made it difficult. The blanket fell to the floor. He needed to get her some fucking clothes. Why the hell had he not done so before he'd picked her up?

He knew the reason. He'd been scared out of his mind that something would happen to block him from actually getting his hands on her. He hadn't wanted to risk jinxing this by planning ahead. He'd order her some clothes tomorrow. She could wear his tonight.

He wished he could run her a bath, but that didn't seem

like his best plan right now. No way would he leave her alone, and he refused to take liberties with her for another moment.

"Go to my dresser and open the third drawer," he ordered.

She hurried across the room and did as he asked.

"Good girl. Take out a white T-shirt and bring it back to me."

She pulled one free from the stack, shut the drawer, and shuffled back to him, presenting the shirt. "Would you like me to undress you, Sir?"

He swallowed back his reprimand. "No, Gemma," he said softly as he took it from her. "Lift your arms."

She looked confused but did as he instructed, and he reached up to pull the shirt over her head and tug it down her body. It came to mid-thigh, covering her sufficiently.

Her lip trembled as she stared down at it. "Does my body not please you, Master?"

Jesus. Damon drew in a breath. He grabbed her hips and pulled her between his legs. "I've never seen anyone more beautiful in my entire life, Gemma. But you're not required to expose yourself to me against your will. You won't be sucking me off or fucking me or anything else, either," he nearly growled. He doubted his words sank in.

"Sir?"

"What did I say would happen if you called me anything but Damon?"

She licked her lips.

"Look at me when you respond," he commanded.

She met his gaze. "You would spank me, S..."

Progress.

This was a fucking risk, but he was out of ideas. He couldn't stand to let her continue to call him by anything other than his name. She could not spend her days *yes, Sirring* him. He'd lose his mind. It literally hurt.

He reached for her hips and brought her to one side of his

lap before carefully lowering her over his thighs. "Clasp your hands at the small of your back, Gemma," he ordered.

She was breathing heavily, but she did as he requested.

Damon set his hand over hers, holding them in place. He pushed his T-shirt up to expose her fucking sexy bottom. And then he palmed it. "Why am I going to spank you, Gemma?" He needed to be sure she understood and stopped the behavior.

She was so fucking submissive. Or was that learned? Forced? He couldn't be sure, but she had calmed since he'd taken her over his knees. She wasn't as stiff.

"I'm not allowed to call you Sir or Master," she whispered as if he'd asked her to jump from a plane. The concept was that foreign to her.

"That's right. Where will your eyes be when you speak to me, Gemma?"

"On yours, Sss... Damon."

"Good girl. I'm going to spank you so you remember."

"Yes, S... Yes, Damon."

Progress. He thought. Maybe.

Damon had dreamed of spanking this sexy ass many times in the past. Every time she'd given him sass while she'd sunbathed by the pool in that fucking revealing thong thing she'd worn. He used to toss and turn at night, wondering what her skin would look like if he swatted it a dozen or so times with his palm.

At the time, he'd visualized insisting she address him respectfully as Sir. My, how the tables had turned.

He lifted his hand and brought it back down, warming her up with a gentle swat.

She flinched but didn't try to get free. She'd undoubtedly been trained to accept her punishments without complaint.

What the fuck am I doing?

Damon lifted his palm and swatted her again.

Her whimper and the way she squirmed made his cock hard.

Down, boy. You are not going to come out to play.

He increased the pressure and spanked her several more times, counting in his head until he reached ten.

Gemma was panting, and she drew her knees together tightly, pulling them up against him.

Damon rubbed her warm bottom. He had no idea if he should be spanking her or not. What would a psychologist say? But he knew he needed to find a way to reach her and change her behavior until she understood she was a free woman. If spanking worked, he would use the tool.

He pulled the T-shirt back over her warm bottom and turned her over gently until she was sitting sideways on his lap.

She was trembling as she pressed her thighs together again. "That's it, Sir?" She stiffened and then lifted her gaze to his, eyes wide. "I'm sorry. Damon."

He chuckled.

She flinched. "You're…laughing at me?" Her brow was furrowed in confusion.

He forced himself to rein in his expression. "Yes, baby. It was kind of funny that you obviously didn't think my punishment was enough. And apparently, it was ineffective because you immediately called me Sir again."

Her breath hitched. "I'll do better…Damon."

He kissed her forehead because fuck if he could resist. She was goddamn cute, all flustered and confused. "What did you think of your first spanking?" he asked.

She licked her lips. "It, uh…" She wiggled on his lap. Was she aroused? That would explain the way she'd clenched her thighs together, and still was.

"Shall I spank you harder next time?" he asked.

Her cheeks turned pink. "I don't know, S—"

He lifted a brow. "Maybe you enjoyed having my palm on your bottom?"

She pursed her lips and lowered her gaze. Bingo. And Lord have mercy. He was not going there right now. Best to change the subject.

He lowered his gaze to the fucking collar around her neck. When he slid his hands up to investigate it, she held her breath. It was a simple belt-type buckle. "I'm going to take this off, baby."

Her hands flew to her neck. "Why? Do you want me to wear a different one instead?"

He frowned. "No. I don't want you to wear a collar at all. You're not a slave."

She blinked. "I am. I'm your slave." Her lip trembled. "You're displeased with me. You don't want me to wear it because I've misbehaved." Tears welled up and tracked down her cheeks.

Damon swallowed past the lump in his throat. "No. Gemma..." He lifted her face and swiped her tears with his thumbs. "I'm not displeased. You've done nothing wrong. I don't want that man's collar on you. May I please remove it?"

She was shaking now. "Will you replace it with yours?"

He gritted his teeth, inhaling slowly. It seemed important to her. He couldn't imagine there would ever come a day when he would collar this woman. It would likely never seem right. But if it calmed her, he would agree for now. "I don't have a collar for you in my home, Gemma, but you can't wear this one. It belonged to another man. If you want me to collar you some day in the future, we can discuss it again. For now, this one must go."

He kept his voice firm for that last part. He could bend on a lot of things to help her transition, but not that fucking collar. It was royally pissing him off. He didn't want to see it another second around her slender neck.

"Yes, Sir," she murmured.

He ignored the honorific. It was at least better than Master. It was clearly going to take some time to break her of the habit. She'd probably been referring to every man around her as Sir for three years.

Gemma's body shook as he removed the collar and tossed it aside. She rubbed her neck and held her hand there.

"Feel better?" he asked.

"Feels weird. Like I'm naked, Sir." She lifted her gaze. "Damon."

"You must be exhausted. How about if we get some sleep?" He lifted her off his lap and set her on her feet. When he stood, he took her hand and led her to the bathroom.

She waited for further instructions as he opened a drawer and pulled out a new toothbrush. He tore it open, put toothpaste on it, and handed it to her. "Brush, baby."

While she did so, he did the same, and then he rinsed and grabbed a hand towel.

Gemma kept brushing, glancing at him every few seconds until he realized she was waiting for permission to stop.

His chest was fucking tight, and he suspected it was going to get tighter in the coming days. "Rinse, baby." He took the toothbrush from her and handed her a cup.

After she rinsed her mouth and turned off the water, Damon dried her hands and lips. "I'll step outside so you can use the toilet."

When he turned to walk out and give her privacy, she said, "Alone, Sir?"

His breath hitched, and he was glad he wasn't facing her because flames came out of his ears. He had to school his face before he turned back to face her. "Yes. You will use the bathroom anytime you feel the need, Gemma. You don't need my permission nor my supervision."

She glanced at the toilet as if his words were ludicrous. She took a few breaths. "You don't want to watch me, Sir?"

"No." *But I do want to kill some people with my bare hands.*

"Okay," she whispered, not moving. "I'll be quick."

"Take your time, baby. Take as long as you'd like." He stepped out of the bathroom and pulled the door closed, leaning against it to take several deep breaths. *Fucking fuck.*

CHAPTER SIX

Damon quickly changed out of his clothes and pulled on a pair of sleep pants while he waited, trying to bring his blood pressure down. What kind of fucking animals watched her pee?

He ran a hand through his hair and took a deep breath as the toilet flushed and then the water turned on. She opened the door and stepped into his room less than one minute after he'd left her. Apparently, she'd been given very little time to piss.

She was still wearing his T-shirt, but she nevertheless stood at attention, hands at her sides, face forward, eyes downcast, shoulders back.

"You need sleep, Gemma," he said gently. "You have two choices. I can put you in a guest room in your own bed, or you can sleep in here with me. Personally, I'd rather you stayed with me so I can keep an eye on you, if you don't mind."

She glanced around the room. "In here, Sir?"

"Yes. Unless you'd rather use a guest room," he reminded her.

"Do you have a cot, Sir?"

Damon drew in a breath. "No."

"The floor is fine, Sir."

Fuck.

Damon shook his head. "You're not sleeping on the floor. Gemma, you can share my bed. I promise I won't violate you. If you'll let me, I'd like to hold you. That's it."

Her lip trembled.

What have I said wrong now?

"Am I not appealing to you, Sir?"

Damon groaned internally. "There is no woman on earth more gorgeous than you, Gemma. But I'm not an animal. We're not having sex. You're not obligated to offer yourself to me."

Her voice shook as she spoke again. "Why did you buy me then, Sir?"

He dragged in another heavy breath. "To set you free, Gemma. No one should own another human being."

She looked confused and opened her mouth several times but didn't speak.

"Come." He reached out a hand and motioned for her to approach the bed as he pulled back the covers.

When she got close enough, he lifted her off the floor and settled her in the center of the bed, meaning to keep her close. He froze when she spread her legs about two feet wide and settled her arms away from her body several inches.

Damon climbed up next to her and sat, looking down at her. He'd just told her they weren't having sex, and yet she looked like she expected him to climb between her legs and fuck her like she wasn't even a living being.

"Gemma..."

She met his gaze.

"We're not having sex."

"Okay, Sir," she murmured.

"What are you doing? Why are you lying like that?"

She gave him another blank stare as if he were from another planet. "Aren't you going to restrain me?"

He couldn't begin to wrap his head around this new development. "Why would I restrain you?"

"For sleep."

His heart stopped. Completely. He was going to need a defibrillator if this kept up. The mother-fucking, cock-sucking piece of scum who'd held her for three years and trained her to let leave of her humanity wasn't going to need one though because when Damon was done beating the man to near death, he would stab his limbs and cut off his dick and gouge out his eyes and cut out his tongue before he let him bleed to death.

He needed clarification right now. "You've been sleeping on a cot with your wrists and ankles shackled to the bed?"

"Yes, Sir," she murmured.

"Why?" The word slid out before he could stop it.

She answered him anyway. "My pleasure was saved for you, Master."

Damon stopped breathing again. They fucking spread her open and restrained her so she couldn't touch herself in the night?

He had two choices: start throwing things or change the subject. He opted for number two. "What's rule number one?"

She flinched. "I'm not permitted to call you Master, Sir."

"And what's the punishment?"

"A spanking, Sir."

"Are you allowed to call me Sir?"

"No, Sir." She gasped. "Damon."

"Flip onto your tummy, Gemma," he ordered.

She immediately did as he told her. The only times she was

animated were when he gave her an order. It was like she was programmed to obey him, and anything that didn't fit into that mold confused her.

Damon lifted her hips and slid a pillow under her so her bottom would be higher. He pushed the T-shirt up her back and palmed her sexy cheeks. They were still pink from the ten swats he'd given her before, but she could take a lot more. Ten was nothing. He hadn't even struck her hard.

If she were any other submissive, he would force her to spread her knees, but he wouldn't demand that of her. The exposure didn't feel appropriate.

Damon gave her a warmup swat on one cheek and then the other. "Turn your face toward me, baby."

She set her cheek on the pillow, the curtain of her hair covering her eyes.

Damon lifted the thick locks and draped them over to the other side of her. "Look at me while I spank you."

"Yes, Sir."

He gave her a hard swat that made her flinch. Her eyes widened. "I'll spank you all night if you don't call me by my name."

"I'm sorry...Damon."

"That's better."

"It's hard. I don't understand."

He smoothed his hand up her bare back under the cotton shirt, liking the way she shivered. "I know, baby. I'm going to help you understand. May I continue?"

"Yes, Damon."

"Good girl."

She might have almost smiled when he praised her. He'd do it all day if it made her smile. He'd missed her smiles more than anything.

He peppered her bottom and her thighs all over, glancing at her face often. When he stopped, she moaned.

Fuck me.

Damon dropped down onto his side next to her and rolled her toward him so that he could hold her against himself, chest to chest. He brushed a loose lock of hair from her face and wrapped his arms around her, holding her tightly.

He kissed her forehead and her cheeks, not daring to touch her lips.

She squirmed against him, and then surprised him. Her eyes were clear and lustful when she spoke. "I used to dream of you spanking me like that."

He sucked in a breath. *Yes. Fuck. Me.* And then he grinned. "Did you, now?"

"Yes." Her cheeks were pink again. "I avoided you outright because I didn't want you to get fired, but I still tried to tempt you by wearing very little when you were around. It was immature."

My God. Here she is. Gemma. His Gemma. The woman he'd met four years ago. How long could he keep her? How long before she slid back into her slave brain.

She was finally staring at him as if she fully recognized him and understood where she was and who she was with.

He needed to make a confession too. "I dreamed of spanking that sexy ass too, baby." He stroked his hand down to cup her warm butt cheek, loving the way she squirmed. "I was too old for you, and your father would've lost his shit, so I never made a move, but I wanted to, and I nearly died when I thought you'd been killed. I searched every room. It scared the fuck out of me to realize you'd been taken, but at least I knew you were alive."

She shook her head. "I'm not. I died that day."

He wanted to scream on behalf of the amazing, vibrant woman who'd had her youth stolen from her. "You didn't. You're right here. I've got you. You're safe now."

"I'm not that girl. I don't remember her." Her voice was so sad, but she was lucid. She was in the here and now.

"We'll find her. Together. And bring her back." He nearly choked, holding back his emotions.

"She's gone," Gemma whispered.

Damon squeezed her ass and then gave it a swat, making her yelp.

"Hey," she cried out.

"See? She's right here. She's not gone."

She stared at him for several long seconds. "I thought about you when I dared let myself dream."

Damon leaned his head against hers. "I thought about you every fucking day, and I spent every hour looking for you until I finally found you." He prayed she would know something about where she'd been kept to help take that fucker down, but he wouldn't burden her with questions yet.

"You bought me," she murmured in awe.

"I only did so to get you back."

"Why?"

Oh damn. That was a loaded question. Was she ready for the answer? The truth? "You didn't deserve to be taken like that. You were innocent and young and full of life."

She narrowed her gaze, and he loved the feistiness behind her eyes. "That's not a good answer, Damon."

He smiled. "No. It's not."

"Why did you buy me?" she insisted.

"Because you're mine."

She sighed heavily as she ducked her head to flatten her forehead against his chest. "I'm broken, Damon. I'm not that girl."

"You *are* that woman, and we'll fix you. Together. You've been so brave for so long. You didn't let him take your soul. I'm sorry it took so fucking long to find you, but I've got you now, and I will help you mend."

"Was my dad a bad man?" she asked his chest.

Damon hesitated.

She lifted her face and met his gaze again. "Just tell me."

"He wasn't anywhere near as bad as the man who kidnapped you. He didn't buy and sell humans."

"He was a drug and ammunitions dealer, wasn't he?"

"Yes. But those don't rank anywhere close to human trafficking. How did you know?"

"I suspected he did illegal things to amass his money, but Master J told me over and over when he first kidnapped me. He told me my father was a very bad man, and it was too bad he was dead, but I would pay for his crimes."

Damon gripped her closer, if that was even possible. "Master J lied." *Who the fuck is Master J?* "You realize he is the scum of the earth, right?"

"Yes." She snuggled in closer, and he thought she might have fallen asleep, but finally, she whispered, "Thank you for rescuing me. I'm not sure I can be fixed, but I'm grateful for your efforts."

He kissed the top of her head.

"I'm going to call you Sir because it's ingrained in me."

"I'm going to spank your bottom because I enjoy it and you do, too." He hoped he wasn't crossing a line. "Maybe when I swat your cute butt, it will help jar you and remind you you're not a slave."

She squirmed against him. "I think I like it when you spank me. It's our thing. It makes me feel closer to you and not to Master J. It makes me feel…other things, too. Is that weird?"

"No, baby. It's normal. I know plenty of women who misbehave in order to get their bottoms spanked by their Dom." He smiled.

"Would you spank me again now, Sir?"

Oh, she was wicked. How fucked up was this?

"It makes me feel alive," she confessed.

"I think it makes you feel horny," he pointed out.

"That, too." She squirmed against him. "When you imagined spanking me, did you also think about touching me?"

"Every fucking time, Gemma," he admitted, holding her gaze. "I've wanted to slide my fingers through your pussy for years." Why lie to her?

"Will you? Will you spank me and then touch me? Please, Damon."

He couldn't deny her anything. "Are you sure? You're sliding in and out of reality. I'm not sure you're capable of making decisions you won't regret later."

She shook her head. "I'm clear right now. In your arms. I remember. I want you to touch me."

"I'm not going to have sex with you," he stated.

"Will you use your fingers?" She rubbed her body against his. "Please. I need you to touch me. No one has touched me in three years. I thought I was hallucinating when I inhaled your scent. I thought I made it up in my mind. I willed the man to be you, and then it was you, and I wasn't sure. It smelled like you, and then you whispered in my ear and it sounded like you. I couldn't believe it. I still think I'm dreaming."

"It's me, baby. I'm yours. Good thing I never switched cologne."

She graced him with yet another smile. "Good thing I remembered it."

"No one has touched you? Is that for real?"

"Yes. We weren't permitted to touch ourselves either."

He wasn't going to ask more questions about her captivity tonight, but he would. Tomorrow. In the light of day.

"Please, Damon. If this is a dream, I want to come before I wake up. I don't even care if I get punished for two days in the kennel for having an orgasm in my sleep. It will be worth it."

Damon closed his eyes. *Don't think about that kennel. Give her what she needs.*

"I don't have to spank you to get you off, baby." His voice was gravelly.

"I want you to. I like how it makes me feel. I like the feel of your palm on my naked butt. It's a rush like nothing I've ever experienced."

"Okay." Damon eased her out of his arms and rolled her carefully to her belly. "Draw your knees up under you. Lift your bottom in the air."

She scrambled into the position.

"Good girl."

She shuddered when he praised her, setting her forehead on her palms.

"Spread your knees, Gemma." He pushed the T-shirt up her body, far enough that it gathered at her shoulder blades and exposed the swell of her breasts.

He loved this position. Every swat would cause her tits to drag against the mattress while her pussy clenched with need.

"Please, Sir," she taunted as she thrust her sexy ass back into his palm.

"Such a naughty girl," he teased, hoping no one had called her that.

She didn't flinch, so he assumed naughty girl was now on the approved list.

Damon lifted his palm and spanked her for the third time since they'd arrived. It was nerve-wracking. He would have to unpack his feelings about this odd arrangement later. For now, he was giving Gemma what she'd asked for.

This time, he spanked her farther down her thighs and concentrated on the sweet spot where her butt cheeks met her thighs.

Gemma gasped. When her body stiffened, Damon set his free hand on the small of her back and reached between her legs. A quick drag through her folds told him she was soaked.

She moaned long and loud, wiggling her sweet bottom.

Damon didn't make her wait. He found her clit and rubbed it hard.

Gemma lifted her head off the cradle of her hands and cried out. Her back arched, and her legs shook. She was so fucking beautiful.

She was his. With the caveat that she also had freewill and could walk out the front door at any time. He would support her and help her any way he could if she chose to leave.

She was here now, though, and he'd never seen anything more gorgeous than Gemma Romano rocking into his hand as he rubbed her clit until she came.

He'd waited a lifetime for this, and he didn't blink. He didn't want to miss a moment of her first orgasm at his touch. He'd give anything to also be the *last* man to touch her pussy, but that was a topic for another day.

He didn't penetrate her. He was confident nothing had been inside her pussy in three years, so even if she'd had a king-sized dildo in her previous life, she would be tight. He wouldn't fill her pussy with even a finger without discussing it with her first.

Sated and shaking, Gemma dropped onto the mattress, her breathing heavy, her hair a wild halo around her face and shoulders and pillow.

She was grinning when he brushed the thick locks away again. "Thank you," she managed.

He leaned over and kissed her. "Any time."

She groaned as she rolled into his arms. He gathered her back against his chest, ignoring the cock between his legs. He'd gotten some earlier even though that had been against Gemma's will. Still, it wasn't his turn.

Damon eventually reached behind himself to turn off the light on the nightstand, and then he snuggled her and thanked God he finally had her. No matter what she needed, he would make it happen.

She was his. She was here in his bed. He wanted to stay awake and stare at her all night, but he was exhausted and let sleep drag him under.

CHAPTER SEVEN

"No. No, no, no. Please... *No*."

"Shh. Gemma. Baby, I'm right here. I've got you. You're safe."

Gemma's heart was racing as that voice filtered into her mind. She was dreaming. About Damon. It was so vivid. She could even smell him and feel his touch. He was holding her, his arms wrapped around her.

She didn't want to wake up. "No... Please..." she begged, suddenly realizing the sound was out loud. Her own voice.

She stiffened, knowing she would be punished for speaking out of turn, and then she gasped. Something was wrong. She wasn't on her cot. She wasn't restrained. Her arms were tucked against her chest. That was forbidden. Had she fallen asleep somewhere other than her cot? Her eyes popped open as fear seeped into her.

"Gemma."

The commanding voice made her jerk to sitting. She scanned the room, recognizing nothing.

"Gemma." The voice was softer this time. "Look at me."

She lowered her face to find someone staring up at her.

She was on a bed in a luxurious room, and a man was next to her.

Suddenly, her mind started piecing it all together. The auction. The presentation. The sale. She'd been sold to a new Master. This was him.

She scrambled to her knees, intending to properly present herself, but he stopped her, hauling her back down next to him.

"Gemma. Look at me," he insisted again. "Eyes on mine."

She met his gaze, heart racing faster. "Damon?"

He smiled. "Good girl. Take a deep breath. You're safe."

"Safe..." What did safe even mean?

He smoothed the hair back from her forehead as she got her breathing under control. "You were having a dream."

"It was about you," she blurted before she could think to stop herself. She lifted a hand to touch his face. "Am I still asleep?"

"No." He smiled. "You're awake. You're in my home. You're safe."

She drew in a deep breath and let it out slowly. Maybe he was right. She hoped so. She glanced around again. The sun was up. It was bright in the room. He hadn't shut the blinds last night.

"What time is it? I'm not allowed to sleep this late."

"You're allowed to sleep as late as you'd like, baby." He stroked her cheek.

What was he talking about? She needed to get up and do her tasks. "I'm sorry, Sir. It won't happen again." She wiggled free of him and slid off the side of the bed. "I'll fix your breakfast." She glanced down at her body, covered in a T-shirt that hung halfway down her thighs.

She yanked it over her head immediately, embarrassed to have covered herself. "Permission to fix your breakfast, Sir."

Damon... It was Damon. He rose and came toward her,

snagging the T-shirt on his way. When he reached her side, he eased the shirt back over her head and helped her stick her arms through the holes.

When he was done, he lifted her chin. "You're not fixing me breakfast. You will come to the kitchen with me and sit on a stool while *I* cook for *you*. Understood?"

She gasped. "I'm trained to—"

He covered her mouth, stopping her mid-sentence. "I'm going to retrain you, Gemma. You're not a slave. We're going to erase that notion from your head."

Not a slave... She blinked as his hand lowered from her mouth.

"Look me in the eye," he demanded.

She forced herself to do as he commanded even though it went against every grain in her body. She wasn't permitted to look at Master. She wasn't permitted to speak out of turn. She wasn't permitted to wear clothing.

She swayed a bit to one side, and Damon caught her, his hands on both biceps. "Keep your eyes on mine."

She tried. It was so hard. So confusing. Why did he want her to look at him?

Damn, he was gorgeous. Flashes of the past came to the forefront. She'd lusted after him when he'd worked for her father. She used to make excuses to come into her father's office and hound him to no end when she knew Damon was in there.

Sure, she'd ignored him entirely as far as he or her father had known, but she'd done so to protect him from her father's wrath. Any man she'd flirted with had ended up fired. It had infuriated her at first, but after about three men, she'd realized she was ruining their lives with her antics and had stopped making eye contact with anyone on the property.

Except Damon. Sometimes, she'd looked at him when he hadn't realized it. Sometimes, she'd stared. She'd known his mannerisms. She'd known how his biceps had flexed when he'd set his elbows on the desk. She'd known how well he'd filled out his pants with his thighs when he'd taken a break to stretch his body out. She'd known the furrow of his brow when he'd concentrated.

She reached up with a trembling hand and touched his brow now, rubbing that crease. "You're really here," she murmured.

"Yes, baby." He wrapped his hand around hers at his temple and brought her fingers to his lips, kissing them.

"You bought me." She was pretty sure she'd confirmed that fact with him a dozen times already, but he didn't seem annoyed.

"I rescued you the only way I could, Gemma." His patience was unwavering. His hand slid down to her butt to pull her closer.

She winced. "You spanked me."

He cocked his head to one side and narrowed his gaze, but he looked like he was going to laugh. "You begged me to."

"Oh." *Right. I did.*

"You touched me," she whispered, remembering the feel of his fingers between her legs.

"Mmm-hmm." He kissed her forehead and slid his lips to her ear, cupping the back of her head. "You begged me to do that, too."

She shivered and allowed herself to smile. "I liked it." Her voice sounded rough.

He chuckled. "I noticed." He spun her around. "Go use the bathroom, baby." He gave her butt a pat.

She hesitated. "You aren't coming with me?"

"No. I told you last night that you can pee without me. You can have privacy any time you want it. I might watch you like a hawk for a while because I'm worried about you, but I'm not going to watch you pee, Gemma."

"What if I touch myself too long while I'm wiping?" she challenged. The entire conversation sounded odd to her ears, but she was struggling to wrap her head around this unexpected turn of events.

I'm in Damon's home. He bought me, but he's not my Master.

Damon seemed flustered by that last question. He sat back down on the edge of the bed and dragged her between his legs, meeting her gaze. "I'm going to say some things, and you're going to listen. Later, I'm going to say them again because you're going to forget. But that's okay. I'll say them a million times until you believe me."

She bit into her bottom lip, holding his gaze even though it was difficult. She hadn't looked a man in the eye in three years.

"You are not my slave. I do not own you. I bought you to free you from that madman."

"But..."

He gripped her biceps and shook his head. "No. That's it. Now, I'll freely admit, I'm a Dominant. That's who I am. But I've never once touched a woman in any way without her permission. I won't spank you or fuck you without your permission."

"What if I'm bad?" Her head was spinning.

"You're not bad. You'll never be bad. No one has the right to control another person against their will for any reason."

She was struggling to follow him. There were moments when he made perfect sense, and then her previous Master's voice would come to her, and she would hear him overriding Damon's rules.

"If we lived in an alternate universe, one in which you were mine by choice and had never been kidnapped, I would probably Dominate you in every way. You would most likely have submitted your will to me of your own accord because I would've made you crave that submission more than your next breath."

She gasped. His words were confusing.

"But we were dealt a different hand, baby. And now, we have to play it blindly without knowing the rules of the game. One day at a time."

"Okay." She wasn't sure what she'd agreed to, but it seemed like he needed her to understand.

He sighed. "As far as the bathroom is concerned, I'd ask that you not lock the door for a few days until I'm certain you're stable enough that you won't scare the fuck out of me. But I won't open it without knocking and giving you fair warning. Okay?"

She nodded slowly. He was going to let her pee alone. "How will you know if I touch myself?" That was a hard rule. The punishment was severe. She shuddered.

Damon winced. In reaction to what? Her shudder? Or her words? She wasn't sure. He drew in a breath. "If..." He let that word hang for a moment. "If, we were in a committed relationship in which you'd agreed to submit to me of your own accord, I would probably not permit you to masturbate, baby. That's how I'm wired."

"I won't," she blurted out.

He groaned. In frustration. Yes, frustration. Because she wasn't understanding. He shook his head. "We're not in that sort of relationship, Gemma. We may never be. I can't predict the future. For now, you may do whatever you please. If you want to go into the bathroom and rub your pussy until you make yourself come, I won't stop you."

She flinched. She used to do that. Often, after she'd met him. She used to lock the bathroom door, sit in the whirlpool tub, and rub her clit until she came to visions of Damon touching her.

That was a lifetime ago. It seemed like it was a different life. Not hers.

She had the urge to cross her arms, but that was never ever permitted, so she fought it and fisted her hands at her sides instead. A coping mechanism she'd developed over time to fight the instinct to cover herself. The small cuts that had often ended up marring her palms had been nothing compared to the punishments she'd received for covering her tits.

"Gemma." The firm tone shook her back to the present.

Damon gripped her hips. "You left me for a moment."

She nodded. She was going to do so often. It was unavoidable. She couldn't stop it. Her training was so ingrained in her. There was no way to fight it.

He narrowed his gaze on hers again. "I will not restrain you or ask you not to touch yourself. Understood?"

She nodded. That's what he needed from her.

"Are you going to masturbate?"

She shook her head rapidly.

He chuckled and pulled her in for a hug. "One day you will, baby. One day." When he leaned her back again, he turned her toward the bathroom. "Use the bathroom, Gemma. I'll be in the kitchen."

She wandered into the bathroom, hesitating in the doorway.

"Close the door, baby," he ordered.

She took a deep breath, shut the door, and stood shaking in the middle of the huge, modern bathroom. Other than thirty seconds last night to pee, she hadn't been alone in three years.

No. That wasn't true. She'd been left alone in solitary confinement many, many times, but even though she'd nearly lost her mind a few times, she'd known she was not really alone. Someone had always watched her.

She jerked her gaze up to the corner of the room, spinning to take in every corner. Did Damon have cameras in his bathroom?

Maybe she was being paranoid. No. She wasn't. People like Damon had cameras everywhere. He may have told her he didn't care if she touched herself, but he would surely be watching.

Master J had cameras in every corner of every room of his house. He'd also kept an ankle monitor on all his slaves so he could track their every movement. The chip in the device had been so specific that he would know if one of them strayed too close to a door or a bathroom.

They'd had specific tasks to achieve every day and rules to follow. Breaking the rules had meant punishment. Every time Gemma had been punished, it chipped away at her soul, so she'd decided almost two years ago to behave at all times. Obeying the rules was easier than suffering the repercussions.

Gemma had convinced herself in the first year that if she ever escaped the living hell that was her life, she would need all her brain cells. If she'd spent many more days in that kennel in the basement, she would have ended up in a straight jacket instead of living life.

She shuddered as she rushed toward the toilet, relieved her bladder, and then headed for the sink. After she washed her hands, she faced herself in the mirror and gasped. Her eyes went wide.

She almost didn't recognize herself. It was still her, but it wasn't. Her hair was a dank tangle of locks that hadn't been combed or well-cared for very often. Her skin was pale. There were circles under her eyes that would probably haunt her for the rest of her life.

Her eyes looked lifeless as if she were a corpse, making her shift her gaze away. She was shaking so badly the room started spinning. She had to grab onto the counter to keep from falling.

I can't do this. I'm not strong enough.

She'd given up hope of being freed so long ago that she'd slipped into another dimension and sort of left her body. She was a robot on autopilot. It had become her survival mechanism. Routine. Rules. Obedience. Day in and day out. She'd left her body so long ago that she didn't remember who she was.

Her legs wouldn't hold her up, so she slid to the floor, afraid if she didn't, she would faint and hit her head on the tile. Damon would be out of his mind if he found her dead in his bathroom from a concussion.

She pulled her knees up to her chest and hugged them, lowering her forehead to her knees. She took deep breaths. It felt so weird to be wearing a shirt. The material felt odd against her skin. It was physically hurting her.

Finally, she stretched out, reached for the hem, and pulled the shirt over her head. She felt more herself after she dropped it to the floor next to her.

How fucked up was she that she breathed easier now that she was naked and exposed? Damon was probably watching her through several cameras. She hadn't noticed where they were located, but she was sure they existed.

Even her father had had cameras in nearly every room of the house. He'd said they were for protection. She'd believed him. She'd made sure there were none in her bedroom or attached bath, but the rest of the house had been monitored at all times.

Master J had been blatant about his cameras. Not only had they been obvious with their flashing red lights in every corner, but sometimes, he'd set them up on a tripod directly in front of a slave who was in deep trouble and filmed their entire punishment.

Those times had been the worst. Gemma squeezed her eyes closed as if she could block out the memory of being filmed in that kennel. It had happened more than once. It had served no purpose except to intimidate the occupant because no one who'd been punished with kennel days could possibly misbehave while inside the metal box.

Occupants spent that time with their ankles and wrists shackled to the corners. It was horribly uncomfortable. There was very little room to change positions. Mostly Gemma had leaned back on her knees, lowered her butt between her feet, and rested her forehead against the hard metal floor. There had been no way to close her legs or even scratch an itch on her face.

Master J had been creative and devious. His goal had been to break every slave without marring her in any way. The shackles had soft linings in the cuffs. No matter how hard Gemma had tugged, she'd never managed to injure herself.

Besides, the punishment for self-inflicted injuries had been one of the worst.

CHAPTER EIGHT

"Gemma?" Damon's voice was followed by a soft knock. "Baby, are you okay?"

She lifted her face from her knees and glanced at the door. "I'm..." What was she going to say? She certainly wasn't okay.

"Can I come in?"

She nodded and then realized how ludicrous that was. "Yes." Her voice was soft.

Damon opened the door and stepped inside. He looked at her and then the shirt before squatting calmly in front of her.

She was shaking violently now. She met his gaze, remembering his rule. "I can't do this."

He reached out slowly as if she were a scared kitten under the porch. When his hand cupped her face, her tension eased slightly. "You can. You're strong. I'm going to help you."

She shook her head. "I'm not. Every time I close my eyes, I'm back there. I can't let myself believe I'm here with you. It's too scary. I'll be devastated if I find out it was all in my head."

Damon sat in front of her, crossing his legs. "I could pinch you," he teased.

She knew he meant well. His levity was appreciated. He probably had no idea what to do with her. She shuddered at the thought of pinching herself. The idea had crossed her mind more than once, just to prove she was no longer inside Master J's estate.

She lifted her gaze to meet Damon's. "You want to know how fucked up my head is?"

He took a breath. "You can say anything to me, Gemma. Anything. I want to know all your thoughts, baby."

"I'm afraid I'm dreaming, but if I pinch myself and find out I'm still in Master J's estate, I'll be punished for marring my skin."

Damon's breath hitched. "You mentioned Master J last night. Is that what he calls himself?"

She blinked as she realized what she'd said. "We aren't permitted to talk about him or his training center."

Damon scooted closer so his knees were almost brushing her legs. "He will never get his hands on you again, baby. You're mine now, for however long you'll have me. If you want to leave my property, I'll hire bodyguards to keep you safe."

She jerked back, hitting her head on the cabinet door behind her. "I had dozens of bodyguards protecting me at my father's compound, including you. And still, I was taken. You can't protect me."

Damon swallowed and glanced down. "You're right. I'm sorry. I'll regret that I wasn't there to protect you myself for the rest of my life. I shouldn't make that kind of promise now either. I can't predict the future, but for now, I don't think Master J knows who bought you, nor do I expect him to want you back. He got what he wanted."

"Revenge against my father? Money for selling me?" She'd wondered about Master J's motives for years. Why her? She'd wondered if the man had raided her father's compound with

81

the specific intent of kidnapping her or if she'd simply been a bonus.

Damon set his hands on her forearms, which were hugging her legs. "I don't know, baby. Perhaps both. I don't know who Master J is yet. I hope one day I will track him down and extinguish him from the earth. Maybe, I'll get answers then."

She gasped and shook her head. "You can't. Damon, you can't. Please don't try to find him."

Damon gripped her fingers. "Let's not worry about the future, okay? One day at a time. One hour. Right now, I need you to eat." He glanced to the side. "Why did you take your shirt off? Were you going to get in the shower?"

She shook her head. "It...felt weird." But sitting there naked suddenly felt weirder.

"Okay, I'd like you to come downstairs to the kitchen so you can eat. If you're more comfortable naked, I won't complain." He shot her a grin. "However, eventually you might want to start wearing clothes again," he suggested. "We'll order you some things online after breakfast. Okay?"

She glanced at herself and back up at him. "I should wear clothes."

"Yes. Eventually. I gave my staff a few weeks off, so no one will see you in the house, but you'll need to cover yourself when they come back."

"You don't want them to see me naked?" Her lip was trembling. *Is he embarrassed by me? Am I not attractive?* She'd seen herself in the mirror. She looked...wrong. Off. Maybe he thought so, too. But that was her face. Her hair. Her eyes. She didn't think her body was different.

He tugged her hand free from her shin and held it, rubbing her knuckles with his thumb. "I'd rather be the only person who sees you naked, baby. Every inch of you is gorgeous and sexy and perfect, but I don't want to share you with anyone else. Can you do that for me?"

She stared at their combined hands. His was so much larger than hers. She liked the look of him touching her. She also liked the way it felt.

Memorized words flowed from her lips. He didn't seem to know the rules. "Slaves are to remain naked and available for their Master's use at all times. The Master may share the slave with anyone he chooses."

The words grew softer as she spoke. They sounded hollow and oddly absurd. She didn't want to be naked in front of people. It was humiliating and degrading. She'd forgotten that fact.

Suddenly, she jerked her hand free of his and snatched the T-shirt up, covering herself with it.

Damon tipped her chin up. "Eyes on mine, baby."

She met his gaze. It centered her every time. It was weird to look him in the eye. She hadn't looked at anyone's face for so long she'd forgotten how much could be gleaned from an expression.

Damon had so many emotions on his face. Kindness, fear, sorrow, dominance, love, anger... "You're not a slave."

The reminder made her flinch, and she nodded. "I'm not a slave."

He smiled. "That's right. Your name is Gemma, and you're a human being with free will. No one can tell you what to do without your permission." He lifted a brow.

"But you have rules," she pointed out. "You said I can't call you Master."

"That's right. You may not call me Master. That implies I own you, and I don't."

"You'll spank me if I do," she murmured, remembering his rule.

He sighed and ran a hand through his hair. He was frustrated.

"I'm sorry, Sir." She trembled, hating that she'd said something that upset him.

"I'm winging it here, Gemma. Trying to figure out what's best for you and what you need to heal. I feel like you need some rules and structure to help you climb out of the hole you're in. You're used to rules. It's all you know. Technically, I would need your permission to dominate you in any way. I need your consent. But frankly, you aren't in the right frame of mind to consent to anything. In order to help you make different choices and remember who you are and what your rights are, I believe you'll benefit from rules and repercussions. Spanking seems appropriate. I will never strike you hard enough to injure you or leave lasting marks. But I will swat your bottom every time you forget who you are to help you remember."

"Okay." She was trying to keep up. It was hard. She could tell he wasn't sure what to do with her, and she couldn't blame him.

"Can you repeat back to me what you understood, baby?"

"You'll make rules for me. If I'm bad, you'll spank me."

He shook his head. "You're not bad, Gemma. You're relearning. How about mischievous or naughty." He smiled and then winked. He'd called her naughty last night. Apparently, it wasn't a horrible term. He was grinning.

"Naughty." She grinned for some reason. It sounded funny.

He smiled broader. "Did I hurt you when I spanked you?"

She shook her head and shifted her weight as she remembered what had happened when he'd spanked her last night. She'd liked it. It had made her wet.

"Would you like me to spank you again, baby?"

She straightened her spine. "Now?"

"Not now. When you forget the rules." He leaned closer,

holding her gaze. "Do I have your permission to spank you when you break my rules, Gemma?"

She nodded. Her mouth was dry.

"See? That's consent."

Consent... No one had asked for her consent for three years. She'd forgotten it was an option.

He took the T-shirt from her and shook it out. "Lift your arms, baby."

She lowered her knees and did as he told her. The cotton didn't feel as abrasive this time. It was actually soft, and it smelled like him.

"Better?" he asked as he helped her stand.

She glanced at the mirror. "I don't look like me."

He set his hands on her shoulders and faced the mirror with her. "You're so beautiful, baby. Every inch of you. I'm glad he didn't injure you on the outside even though we have a lot of work to do on the inside."

She took a deep breath. The girl in the mirror was all wrong. "I don't remember me."

"Probably because you always wore perfect makeup and had your hair styled." He lifted a heavy section of her hair. "It hasn't been cut in three years," he pointed out. "When you're ready, I'll have a stylist come to the house if you want. A cut and style will make you feel better. And we can order whatever kind of makeup you want."

"I don't remember how to put it on," she whispered.

"It will come back to you." He leaned over and kissed the top of her head. "Let's get food in you and then you can soak in the bath for a while."

She glanced at the tub, longingly. Suddenly, she felt like her skin was crawling from her captivity. "Damon..."

"What?"

"Could I..." She jerked her gaze back, remembering her place. "Never mind."

He spun her around to face him. "Finish your question."

She swallowed. "I shouldn't have been so insolent. I'll do whatever you want."

He shook his head. "Having your own opinions and desires isn't insolence, Gemma. It's independence. Tell me what you were going to say."

She started trembling. What if he told her *no?* Maybe eating first was a rule...

"Gemma, I know what you're thinking. Though, I'd rather you verbalize it. You need to learn to speak up."

She cleared her throat. *He won't hurt me.* No matter what, she knew that, and that was all that mattered. "Please, may I take a bath first?" she asked, her voice wobbling.

"Absolutely." He smiled. "See? Easy." He reached over and turned on the water, feeling it with his hand and adjusting it before putting the stopper in. "I don't have bubbles. If you like those, we'll have to order them. But I do have jets."

She stared at the filling tub, salivating. "I haven't had a bath in three years," she murmured.

He flinched. "You may take as many as you'd like. Sit in here all day if you want. I do have an amazing shower, too." He pointed at it. "Jets coming from all sides and the ceiling. You can set it up however you'd like."

She looked around the glass enclosure as he spoke. "I haven't had a shower either." Words kept tumbling out of her mouth. She couldn't stop them.

Damon ran a hand down his face. She hated the way he stiffened and looked like he was going to break something every time she gave him another detail. She needed to keep her mouth shut.

He tipped his head toward the ceiling and took a deep breath, his hands fisted at his sides. Finally, he lowered his gaze. "How did you..." His question died on his lips as if he couldn't think of what to ask.

She shivered and turned her attention back to the tub, watching it fill.

"Gemma…" His voice was calmer, but he still wanted her to answer him.

She looked at his face again. It was beyond awkward meeting his gaze. He'd insisted, but it didn't come naturally. Would it ever? "I shouldn't have said anything."

He took her shoulders. "Eventually, I want you to tell me every detail. For one thing, it will help you heal to purge things. For another thing, it will help me know who kidnapped you."

She pursed her lips. She didn't want him to know who'd kidnapped her. Even the few things she'd told him had sent him into a rage he could hardly contain. If he had any idea what she'd been through, he would tear the city to shreds. That's how pissed he'd looked.

She didn't want him to risk his life any more than he already had for her. She didn't want to lose him. If he found Master J, the man would kill him, and where would that leave her?

Damon pulled her into his arms, holding her against his chest. He kissed the top of her head. "I'm sorry, baby. I know you hate it when I get angry. I'm trying not to react so violently to everything you say."

She wrapped her arms around his middle. It felt good to hug him. His body was warm, and she loved the way he smelled. His cologne filled her nostrils, and she inhaled it deeply. It calmed her.

When he eased his grip and tipped her back, he spoke again. "I want to know everything, baby. Not all at once, but gradually."

"You can't go after him, Damon."

"You let me worry about that, okay?"

She shook her head. Tears welled up and tumbled down

her cheeks. "I can't lose you. I just got you."

He gripped her tighter. "You won't. I promise."

Tears fell. She shook her head. "Don't look for him. Please."

His hands slid up to her face, and he held her. "I won't do anything without informing you first, baby. I promise. But eventually, I will find him. He has to be stopped. You don't want him to continue kidnapping and selling girls, do you?"

She cringed. She hadn't thought of that. "No."

"Then he has to be stopped."

She nodded slowly. "Let someone else do it."

He set his forehead against hers. "I don't want you to worry about that asshole right now. I'm not going anywhere."

"Okay," she murmured, trying to calm her racing heart. She could argue with him about this again later. It felt weird arguing. She hadn't done it with anyone in so long. It felt... natural. She used to argue with her father all the time. It felt nice to be able to make demands, even if Damon had no intention of granting them. Neither had her father.

Damon leaned down and turned off the water. The tub was full. He came right back to face her. "Answer my question. How did you bathe, Gemma?"

She lowered her head. Might as well tell him. He was obstinate and persistent. He wouldn't stop until she told him. "He used a hose."

Damon flinched. "Outside? It's fucking cold outside most of the year."

She shook her head. "In the basement. Over the drain." But it had been just as cold. There had been no temperature control on the hose. He'd made the slaves stand over the drain, wrists restrained to the ceiling.

She squeezed her eyes shut, trying not to let the memory flood back in. She'd hated the days he'd bathed them. He'd used some sort of liquid soap and his bare hands, running them all over her body before hosing her down with a common garden hose.

It had been cold and humiliating. Over time, she'd forgotten what it was like to wear clothes, so she'd stopped trying to cover her nudity, but wash days had made her want to scream. There'd been something infinitely more violating about having Master J or one of his employees fondle her body. They'd always lingered too long over her breasts and pussy, making her hate them even more.

She was glad Damon didn't ask for more details. She knew he would later, but she didn't have the strength right now.

"Let's get you in the tub," he murmured, his voice low and sad. He lifted his shirt back over her head, took her hand, and helped steady her as she stepped in.

She moaned as she slid under the water. Nothing had ever felt so good in her life. Not that she could remember. Except maybe the orgasm he'd given her last night. That had been pretty damn amazing.

"Do you mind if I stay, baby?" he asked, his voice calm and pleading.

"I don't mind, Sir." She winced. "Damon." She tipped back her head to meet his gaze. It seemed like he trusted her sincerity more when she looked him in the eye. "I like it when you're nearby. It calms me. I start to panic when you're not in the room," she admitted.

He gave a nod. "I prefer to be nearby, too. I'm worried about you." He picked up a bottle of shampoo. "This isn't anything fancy, but it will do. We can order something floral. You always smelled like coconut. Do you still like that scent?"

She hadn't remembered that until he mentioned it. "I don't know."

"We'll order a few scents, and you can choose." He poured shampoo onto his palm. "Would you like me to wash your hair?"

She nodded. She wanted him to erase the other people. Maybe he could if she let him touch her. "Please."

He looked so pleased when he smiled. "Tip your head back to get it wet."

She eased her head into the water, sinking all the way under before rising back out.

He chuckled. "I think you're wet now." He came to the other end of the tub, sat on the wide edge, and gently set his hands on her head.

She closed her eyes and luxuriated in the feel of his kind fingers rubbing her scalp.

"I can do this all day if you want, baby."

"Mmmm. I'm not going to stop you."

He took his time. With each passing minute, she relaxed further. Maybe she was safe. She wanted to believe it.

When he finally finished and helped her ease back to rinse off the bubbles, she stared at him. "Did you really look for me for three years?"

"Yes."

"Why?"

He helped her sit back upright. "I was half in love with you, Gemma. And you didn't deserve whatever was happening to you. I couldn't sleep or eat or even sit still for months. I pulled my hair out by the roots in a total panic. I searched for you because you're a human being who needed rescue. But I also searched for you because I selfishly wanted you for myself."

She licked her lips. Her heart beat faster.

He tipped her chin back. "You're not obligated to return my affections. I hope you know that. I want to help you get your life back. You're free to leave at any time though. You owe me nothing."

"How much did you pay for me?" Why did such odd questions fall out of her mouth all the time?

"Doesn't matter. I would have given my life for you."

"Damon, how much?"

He grabbed the bath soap and held it out. "Would you like to wash yourself?"

She shook her head. "No. I want you to do it." It felt good to be able to speak her mind, but she owed him an explanation. "I haven't washed myself in three years. Other men ran their hands over me. It was humiliating. I want you to replace those memories with *your* hands."

He swallowed hard but somehow managed to not show as much anger as earlier. He surely knew it stressed her out.

"Okay, baby." He picked up a wash cloth, but when she shook her head, he set it back down and poured the soap onto his palms. After building up a lather, he started with her arms, massaging her fingers one by one and working his way to her elbow and then her shoulder.

He took his time, touching every inch of her as if he understood her need for him to wash away the previous men and replace their touch with his own.

It was exactly what she needed, and she couldn't thank him enough for giving her this. Maybe she should have insisted no one ever wash her again, but she wanted Damon's hands on her. She wanted to close her eyes and memorize his touch. He was gentle and careful. Not groping like an animal. Not cackling while he touched her. Not treating her like she wasn't a human being.

He finished between her legs, but he didn't linger or make it sexual. He made it perfect.

When he was done, his breath hitched. "Fuck. Gemma?"

She blinked her eyes open to meet his gaze. "What?"

"You're crying. Did I...?"

She hadn't known she was crying. She lifted her hands and swiped away the tears, shaking her head. "That was exactly perfect."

His shoulders relaxed. "Okay." He pushed a button on the edge of the tub, making the jets come on.

She smiled as she wiped away the rest of the tears and leaned back, letting her body fully submerge in the luxurious warm water. Nothing had ever felt this good. Even the slight roar of the motor was soothing.

"Would you like me to leave so you can soak a while? I can make breakfast and have it ready."

She reached for his hand, dripping water all over him as she gripped his fingers. Her chest tightened. "Please stay."

He nodded and leaned over to kiss her forehead. "Not going anywhere."

She calmed but then started worrying. "I'm asking too much of you. You have things to do. I don't want to be a burden."

He reached under the water to grab her hand, again heedless of the fact that he was getting wet. "You are not a burden. Never. I don't have anything else to do. No other place to go. Nothing. All I care about is you. I'm exactly where I want to be. I don't like the idea of leaving you alone anyway. But I want to respect your privacy at the same time. If and when you want me to bug off, you tell me."

She gripped his fingers under the water and held on, nodding. "Thank you."

CHAPTER NINE

Dressed in another one of Damon's T-shirts, this one black, she let him guide her downstairs. She hadn't seen anything of his house last night. She'd been out of her mind panicking and mostly had her eyes closed. Plus, he hadn't turned on the lights.

It was day now, though, and sun was streaming in from dozens of windows. Damon appeared to like a lot of light. The living room was huge and comfortable. Not formal like her father had preferred.

The sectional looked like someplace she could curl up and nap or read. She had no idea where those thoughts came from since she hadn't napped or read in three years. The colors were earthy browns and greens.

There was a huge flatscreen television over the mantle. She hadn't seen a TV in three years either. She'd sometimes heard what she knew were sounds of shows or news somewhere in the house, but not in rooms she was permitted to enter.

This home was enormous. She glanced at him. "This is a

very nice home. You must have your own money. Why were you working for my father?"

Damon pulled her to his side, holding her close. "My father was wealthy. He owned several properties. He and I didn't see eye to eye. When he died, I sold everything and bought this place. I don't need more than this. Hell, no one does."

"I love it."

"Good." He gave her a squeeze. "Let's get food in you." Holding her hand, he led her through the living room and into the kitchen behind it. Another wall of windows gave her an amazing view of the property, including a pool, huge older trees, and inviting places to sit.

She dropped his hand to step closer. "Damon…"

"Pretty, huh?"

"Beautiful."

"Is there anything you don't like for breakfast? Or can I just start cooking?"

She turned and hurried toward him. "I can do it. I'm… trained." She let that last word trail off.

He grabbed her by the waist and deposited her on a stool at the enormous island. "You will not cook for me. You will not clean my home. You will not lift a damn finger. Understood?"

She drew in a breath. "I used to like cooking."

"Okay. We can revisit that possibility another day. Not now. Not until I'm sure you aren't doing so because you were trained to wait on me." He turned toward the fridge, pulled out the orange juice, and held it up. "OJ?"

Her mouth watered. "Please."

"Now, answer my question. What foods don't you like?" he asked as he poured her a giant glass and slid it toward her, leaving the carafe where she could reach it.

"I was never a picky eater. I don't remember what I like, but I never want to see oatmeal again in this life."

He winced and then nodded. "I'll get all the oatmeal out of the house."

"Maybe keep it for cookies?" she suggested, managing to smile. It was shocking how light he could make her feel. She was gradually starting to feel almost slightly human.

He chuckled. "My housekeeper makes amazing oatmeal, chocolate-chip cookies."

Her stomach grumbled.

"I'll consider that a *yes*." He pulled more things out of the fridge, listing them off. "Eggs, bacon, pancakes?"

Syrup... Another grumble. "That sounds so good."

"Coffee? Tea? I know you used to drink coffee that was more like cream and sugar with a splash of brown in it," he teased.

She blinked for a moment. "You know me better than I know me."

He shrugged. "I have a good memory for all things Gemma."

"I don't remember Gemma well at all," she whispered.

"Good thing you have me to remind you then, huh?"

She nodded. Emotions welled up. If she tried to speak, she would cry again.

He started the bacon and then grabbed a box of tissues from the end of the counter and brought them to her, lifting her hand to his cheek. "You never need to hold back or force yourself to be strong with me, baby. Cry if you want. I totally understand. Cry all day. Cry every day. Get it out. I'll hold you and wipe your tears."

She nodded again and reached for a tissue as he kissed her forehead.

She watched his every move as he cooked. He was gorgeous

and sexy, and she hadn't watched anyone doing even the most mundane tasks in so long. She'd never been idle unless she was standing, kneeling, or lying in one of the many positions she'd gone through every day until she could do them in her sleep.

She didn't want to cry right now, so she dabbed her eyes, wiped her nose, and sucked it all back.

Damon was amazing. The man was doing ten things at once. Somehow in between mixing pancakes, flipping bacon, and frying eggs, he also made her the perfect cup of coffee.

She groaned as she took a sip. "Oh, my God. I remember now." She hadn't had coffee in three years. Or orange juice. She picked that up next. Delicious.

Damon smiled at her over his shoulder, but he also frowned at the same time if that was even possible.

When Damon finally sat down next to her, setting two plates full of food on the counter, he glanced at her drinks and then at her hands. "Drink your juice, baby. You need the sugar. You're shaking."

"Yes, Sir." She reached for it but then flinched when he suddenly grabbed the glass and set it out of her reach.

"Shit. I'm sorry." He looked nervous. "Please forgive me. I shouldn't have ordered you to drink anything. I wasn't thinking. I'm going to make mistakes. I'm treading water just like you."

Now, *he* was shaking.

"Damon?" She was confused.

"Would you like some orange juice, Gemma?" he asked in a rather formal tone.

"Yes. Of course. I told you I did."

He slid the glass back in front of her. "Drink as much as you want, or don't drink it at all. Just…" He closed his eyes and inhaled deeply.

She reached out and touched his face. "It's okay. I get it. You're trying to help me. I'm not offended. I'm just overwhelmed and confused. I was watching you cook, and I forgot to keep drinking. I do want the juice."

He leaned into her palm. "Okay. I'm going to try not to order you around. You don't need that. You need to know that you can make your own choices."

She gave him what she hoped was a teasing grin. "But you have rules, remember? And you said you'd spank me."

He groaned and shot her a return glare. "So far, I've given you two rules. You may not call me Master, and I want you to look me in the eyes. I'm not sure either was a good idea."

"So, you don't mind if I call you Master?" Was she actually being funny? She was shocked by her own words.

His brows shot up. "Did you just make a joke?"

"I think I did."

"Are you planning to call me Master and look down when you talk just so I'll spank you?"

"Yes," she answered without hesitation.

"Then spanking you really isn't a deterrent, is it?"

She slowly shook her head. "No." She squirmed on the stool. She'd enjoyed the feel of his palm on her butt. It had grounded her. Made her feel alive. Plus, he'd been touching her, and she'd enjoyed the way he'd held her hands at the small of her back.

She probably shouldn't have liked it, but she wanted him to do it again.

He pointed at her plate, looking flustered. "Eat."

"Is that an order?"

He chuckled. "Funny girl." Finally, his face grew serious, and he cupped the back of her neck and brought his lips to hers. Not her forehead or the top of her head or her cheek. He kissed her on the lips. It wasn't a long passionate connection. But it was their first kiss, and she was lightheaded when he released her lips.

"I liked that," she whispered.

"I did, too."

"Will you do it again?"

"Eventually." He released her to point at her plate again. "Maybe if you eat your breakfast." He smirked. It was cute and kind of sexy.

She was starting to remember his mannerisms. "Does the length of my next kiss depend on how much food I eat?" She actually smiled now.

Damon flat-out laughed. "I forgot how sassy you could be."

She picked up her fork and took a bite of pancake first. Damon had poured syrup all over the top. She moaned around the bite. "My God. I changed my mind. I don't want to do any of the cooking."

Damon smiled. "I'll cook for you until we die of old age if you want."

She nearly choked on her bite and broke his second rule when she asked him her next question with her gaze on her plate. "Why did you buy me, Damon?"

"I told you I was half in love with you."

"You don't know me. We hardly ever spoke to each other back then." She pushed her eggs around, but Damon took the fork out of her hand, scooped up a bite of egg, and held it to her lips.

She took the bite.

He handed her back her fork. "I know you. I didn't have to talk to you. I listened. You talked a lot. Mostly to sass your father, but I listened when you talked to your friends. I knew what you were studying and reading. I knew what foods you liked and your favorite outfits. I knew you liked to shower at night and often went to bed with wet hair."

She gasped at that last part.

He chuckled. "You announced it, baby."

"Oh. Right." She took another bite when he nodded toward her plate.

"If you keep eating, I'll keep talking."

She swallowed. "Okay."

He continued to eat too, but in between bites, he shared more. "It wouldn't have mattered if I liked you or not. Even if you'd been a bitch I couldn't stand to be around, I would've searched for you. You didn't deserve to be sold into slavery, Gemma. No one does."

"Okay, but now what? I'm not that girl anymore. I don't even know her. You can't know how you might feel about me tomorrow or the next day." She was nervous about this issue. What if she was too much for him? Too much work? Too much trouble? Too fucked up?

He reached over and took her hand. "Gemma, I don't want you to worry about me. I'm solid. Every emotion I ever felt for you flooded back to the surface the moment I set eyes on you last night, and I'm even more sure of my feelings today. I promise you I will never walk away. You will always, for the rest of your life, be able to count on me for anything. That being said, I'm older than you. I knew how I felt three years ago. I was thirty-two. You were twenty. I will never pressure you to stay with me. If at any point it doesn't feel right to you, I will not be angry. I will let you go. You're so young. You have your entire life ahead of you. I want to see you through this stage, but it's more important that I do so as a friend than a lover."

"I wasn't a baby," she countered.

"I didn't say you were," he said softly.

"Did you think I didn't notice you?"

"I was usually in the room. So it was hard not to notice me," he pointed out.

She rolled her eyes.

He chuckled. "Sassy girl with sassy eyes."

"What I mean was I noticed you just as much as you

noticed me. I worked hard to ignore you even more than I ignored anyone else. Did you know that?"

He smiled and squeezed her hand. "I'd hoped, but I couldn't be sure."

"Then you know I didn't want you to get fired. That's why I ignored you. It would've broken my heart if you'd been sent away. Being in the room with you was better than never seeing you at all."

His eyes slowly closed. His lips were turned up. He brought her hand to his mouth and kissed her knuckles.

"And for the record, I was never that sassy. I started that stunt after you arrived. I needed to make shit up so I'd have a reason to barge in and talk to my father, so I started being disagreeable. It worked." She took a bite of pancake, letting that sink in.

When he finished eating, he shoved his plate away and turned his stool to face her. "I need you to understand that I'm going to try not to be bossy with you, but it's in my DNA. I'm a Dominant guy. So it's important for you to know that you don't have to do a damn thing I say, not even if it sounds like an order."

"Okay."

"Yeah? You weren't old enough to understand the components of a Dom/sub relationship, but the first rule is that it must be consensual. If it's not, it's abuse. You're not my submissive—"

"What if I want to be?" she interrupted, feeling bold.

He shook his head. "You can't be. Not right now, Gemma. It's not on the table or up for discussion. You need therapy and help. You can't emerge from three years of intense abuse and slavery and switch to being someone's sub."

"I think it might be easier," she pointed out. "The structure. The rules."

"That may be, but we're not going to do it because it

confuses the fuck out of you. Every time I've given you an order, you've slid back into a headspace I don't like."

"I'm sorry."

"No reason to be sorry. Ever. The point is I want you to know you can counter me on everything I say. You don't have to do a damn thing, even if it sounds like I ordered it. If I tell you to eat your food and you don't like fried eggs, say so. I won't make them that way next time."

She glanced at her plate. "Since you brought it up..." she teased.

"You don't like fried eggs?" He sat up taller, his brows furrowed. "Gemma," he groaned, "why did you eat them?"

She grinned. "I'm kidding. They were perfect and delicious."

He narrowed his gaze. "Don't lie to me."

"I'm not. I doubt I could if I wanted to."

"Promise me you'll think for yourself and counter me if you don't like something I suggest. I might think my request is important and insist you do it anyway, but I'll provide reasons."

"Deal." She wasn't sure she could follow through with this plan. Obeying him was what she'd been trained to do. But it was important to him, so she would try.

CHAPTER TEN

The sound of the doorbell made Gemma's heart race. She grabbed onto Damon's arms, fear climbing up her spine. Piercing fear that threatened to overwhelm her.

The room started spinning. What if Master J had found her and was coming to take her back? She'd rather die. She wouldn't survive going back to him.

Damon leaned closer and held on to her. "Hey. It's okay. It's just the door." He pulled his phone out of his back pocket and tapped the screen. "Shit."

"What?" Now, she couldn't breathe. Whoever it was displeased Damon.

He met her gaze as he stood, taking her with him. "It's just Robert, one of my friends. I forgot to call him when we got home last night. He's probably panicking."

"He knew you bought me?"

"Yes." Damon started walking toward the door.

Gemma held on to him. She didn't want to go to the door, nor did she want a stranger to come into the house. She was in a full panic.

Damon lifted her off the floor, swung her into his arms,

and carried her to the sofa. He settled her in the corner and pulled a throw blanket down over her. After bending down to kiss her lips, he held her chin. "Take a breath. It's going to be okay. Let me answer it before he freaks out."

She pulled the cover tightly around her, shivering under it. An odd modesty she hadn't been permitted for three years came to the surface. She was only wearing Damon's T-shirt. It barely covered her ass. Maybe that's why he'd tucked her under a blanket. He'd said he wasn't going to share her body with anyone.

She held her breath while he opened the front door. She was close enough to hear his greeting. "Robert, I'm so sorry. I forgot to call you." He held the door wider, letting the other man in. Robert was several years older than Damon, with tanned skin and hair. The two of them could have been brothers.

"I've been pacing for two hours. Ella finally told me to come over here. You haven't answered your phone."

"I apologize. I've been kind of busy. I forgot to take my phone out of night mode."

Robert looked around, spotting Gemma on the couch and freezing in his spot. "My God. You were successful."

"Yes." Damon shut the door and rushed toward her.

She appreciated the way he sat next to her and pulled her to his side.

"Gemma, this is my friend Robert. He owns the club I belong to, Roses and Thorns."

Gemma realized she was staring and jerked her gaze down, her cheeks flaming.

She could see Robert inching forward. "So nice to finally meet you," the man said in a very kind voice. He approached slowly.

Gemma couldn't keep her fear at bay. She clenched Damon's arm, wrapping hers around it in a death grip. She realized her reaction wasn't reasonable, but she couldn't stop it.

She was also fighting another problem. Every molecule in her body screamed at her to drop to her knees, spread them wide, and present herself to this guest. No matter who he was, she was trained to service him if her Master commanded it.

She squeezed Damon's arm so tightly she was probably gouging him with her blunt nails, and yet he didn't act the least bit bothered by it.

Robert stopped several feet away and took a seat in the nearest chair, perching carefully on the edge. "I didn't mean to upset you, honey. I'm sorry. I was worried."

Gemma was shaking. It was hard to catch her breath. She knew on some level, somewhere in her head, she'd just had a nearly normal breakfast with Damon. Except for the difficult discussion subjects, she'd felt safe and relaxed her guard.

She couldn't control the fight-or-flight sensation that consumed her now that a stranger had entered the house. Granted, he wasn't a stranger to Damon.

The reasonable corner of her brain that had yet to make a long-term appearance was telling her this man was safe and meant her no harm. He was Damon's friend. Damon wouldn't have let him into the house if he didn't trust him.

No one had asked her to do a thing. She wasn't expected to drop to her knees and suck him off or offer her body to him while Damon watched. The ingrained training to do just that made her instinctive reaction hard to ignore.

Damon's hand came to the top of her head, and he sheltered her, silently holding her face against his chest and stroking her scalp, letting her know it was okay to bury her face.

She was trembling violently. Irrational thoughts wouldn't leave her alone. Thoughts of being spread open and fucked by

this newcomer while her Master held her down and watched
assailed her. She couldn't shake them free.

"You will service your Master any time he demands it."

"If he has guests, you will service them, too."

"Your tight cunt was made to service men."

Gemma jerked her hands to her ears and covered them,
trying to block out the voices. She screamed.

Hands came to her biceps, gripping her, shaking her.
"Gemma, look at me." She heard the voice over the ringing in
her ears, but she couldn't find a way to respond. It felt like she
was trapped inside herself. Whoever Gemma was, she was
buried inside the body of Marigold. She wasn't meant to come
back out. She was gone. Dead. Unreachable.

And yet, a man was calling her name. "Gemma...
Gemma..." It came from far away, and she recognized the
voice. It was a kind voice. A friend. A safe place. She wanted
to look at him but couldn't get to the surface. She was
underwater, drowning, not breathing.

"Gemma," he shouted louder.

Damon?

She suddenly sucked in a deep breath, his scent filling her
senses. It was Damon. If she could just come out of her body,
she could see him, but she was trapped.

Marigold's body was lifted off the couch, and she
screamed again, expecting the inevitable. She knew her place.
She was nothing but a fucktoy. A slave. A useless girl. A
poisonous flower. Tainted. Dirty. Worthless.

Instead of flattening her over the table or on the floor or
the back of the couch, hands settled her on a lap. Arms
wrapped around her, holding her. Lips came to her temple,
kissing her gently.

He was whispering words in her ear, but she couldn't hear
them over the pounding in her heart. She was fighting inside
her body. Trying to get out. She couldn't think about the

man's words. She needed to get out of the dark corner and open her eyes.

"You're safe. I've got you. Please, baby. Please look at me."

He was rocking her gently, soothing her, cradling her, stroking her back. Damon.

Her Damon.

She wanted to see him.

"Breathe, baby. Take another breath for me. You're going to pass out."

She wanted to obey him. He was giving her an order. She was supposed to do whatever he said. He was her Master.

No. Damon was not her Master. No one was. She was free. Why was she still trapped?

Gathering all her strength, she fought to surface and finally burst free of the prison, eyes shooting open and a desperate gasp for oxygen.

"That's a good girl."

Damon. He was staring at her, holding her face with one hand, so she had to look at him.

She held his gaze, knowing it was the only thing that would ground her and keep her in this world. This dimension. He was the only one who knew who she was and could bring her out of herself. Gemma. The girl she'd been before. Before the living hell that became her existence.

"You're safe, baby. No one is going to hurt you."

She swallowed and took another breath.

"That's it. Keep looking at me."

She couldn't, though. She was afraid this wasn't real. Her mind was playing tricks on her. She squeezed her eyes closed and tucked her head down. She wasn't permitted to make eye contact.

"Eyes on mine, Gemma. What's my rule?"

She flinched. He had rules. She was breaking the second

one. She jerked her gaze back to his at the reminder. "Damon…"

"Good girl. What's my rule?"

She licked her lips. "Eyes on yours."

"That's right. What happens if you break the rules?"

"I get spanked." She shivered on his lap, remembering his spankings. They were not deterrents. Not even close. She wanted him to spank her again. She needed him to. It would jerk her free and keep Gemma at the surface. His spankings made her feel alive. Almost whole. They made her feel.

Damon kissed her forehead. "That's right." He rubbed her back again and rocked her.

"Aren't you going to spank me, Sir?"

He stroked her lips. "Yes, but not in front of Robert."

She flinched, sitting up straighter. She'd forgotten there was another man in the room. She didn't dare look in his direction.

Damon held her face and her gaze. "When I spank you, it will always be on your bare bottom so I can monitor how red your skin is. Remember, I told you I won't expose you to anyone else?" He lifted a brow.

She nodded slowly.

"Who gets to see your gorgeous body?"

"Just you, Sir."

"That's right. So, I'll spank you later. I'd like you to turn and look at Robert. You need to face other people. You need to trust that I won't let anyone into this home who would harm you."

She nodded again.

"Be brave for me."

"Okay," she whispered. Finally, she turned her head toward the feet and legs she could see nearby. She stared at the man's loafers and jeans for a moment before lifting her gaze to his face.

He looked concerned but forced a smile. "Nice to meet you, Gemma."

She licked her lips. "Nice to meet you, too, Sir."

Damon rubbed her back. "Good girl. What did I say about calling people Sir?"

"I don't have to."

"That's right. Robert is my friend. He's a Dom, but he's not *your* Dom, and we're not at the club playing. He's just Robert."

"Okay." Her cheeks heated. She'd done the wrong thing. She was embarrassed. She didn't know the right things to say or how to read social cues. It was difficult to read this man's expression, but he was putting off a lot of vibes ranging from pleased to angry. "I'm sorry, Sir." She bit her lip and lifted her gaze toward Damon.

He gave a small chuckle. "It's okay, baby."

Robert ran a hand over his hair. "Damon..." His tone was filled with concern.

"I know," Damon responded.

He knows what?

"You need help. Have you called anyone?"

"Not yet. You're the first person who's come into the house, and judging by how panicked she is, I think she needs some time before I invite a stranger here."

"You need a psychologist. She's been through unimaginable hell."

"I know," Damon agreed.

Gemma stiffened and grabbed his hand, shaking her head. She didn't want a stranger to come here.

"I know some people," Robert said. "Through the club. And Club Zodiac. I bet I can find someone I trust to help you."

"Thank you. I think Jagger knows some people, too."

Damon reached for the corner of the blanket that had fallen from her shoulder and tucked it back around her, cocooning her. This time, it didn't hurt. It was soft, and she felt protected. Surely, that was a good sign. At least she didn't feel the urge to yank off her clothes and drop down onto her knees, naked and exposed for this stranger to inspect.

"What's your immediate plan?" Robert asked.

"She needs clothes. We're going to order some online this morning. Plus makeup and things to help her feel like herself." Damon continued to stroke her back absentmindedly while he spoke.

She loved how he held her and touched her. She wanted to twist in his lap and cling to him. Climb up him. In him. She was only calm when he held her. It would feel even better when he spanked her. She wanted Robert to leave so Damon could spank her.

"Do you think it's a good idea to spank her?" Robert asked gently.

Damon's fingers stiffened on her back. "It seems to help. So far. I'm monitoring her. Don't worry. She wasn't beaten in any way. Her abuse is mostly psychological from what I've gleaned so far. Not physical. The spankings seem to ground her."

"But... Should you be dominating her at all? I'm worried, Damon."

Gemma clenched onto Damon tighter. She didn't like this man interfering. It was grating on her nerves. Could he please just leave?

Damon sighed. "Listen, it's been an intense twelve hours. We're taking it one minute at a time. All I can say is she's calmed by rules and repercussions. I'm taking my cues from her."

"Rules?" Robert groaned.

"Don't growl at me," Damon snapped, making Gemma flinch and burrow into him deeper. "She has two damn rules. They're important. I can't reach her without them." Damon lifted Gemma's chin. "What are our rules, baby?"

She bit her lip for a moment and then found her voice when he lifted a brow. "I'm not allowed to call you Master, and I have to look you in the eyes when I talk."

"Oh." Robert breathed out a sigh of relief. At least, that's what Gemma thought it was.

"I know it's hard to fathom right now, but before you got here, we had a fairly normal breakfast. She's made incredible strides in a few short hours. I've told her repeatedly that she's free, that she owes me nothing, and that she can leave at any time. She's struggling to grasp that she doesn't have to obey me. Obedience is all she knows, it will take time to bring her out of her shell."

"I get it," Robert said softly. "Just be careful. She's fragile."

"I've thought hard about options. Every one of them makes me cringe. I can't simply take her to a hospital. They'd move her to psych. She wouldn't survive. Besides, if I take her anywhere at all, I run the risk of her seller finding out what I've done. If I go to the police, I'll be putting her life in danger. If I walked into a stranger's office for counseling, that person would be obligated to report the crime. If you know someone private who can help us discreetly, we'll consider the option. Not yet, though. She's not ready."

Gemma was shivering, but she liked the way he included her in his statements. "We" would discuss things... It was weird thinking she would be permitted to make decisions, but he'd said so from the very beginning, and he meant it.

She caught Robert nodding even though she didn't look at him directly again.

"You're right," he said. "Will you stay in touch, please? If or when she's ready to meet Ella, I'd love to bring her over. Maybe a female companion would be helpful." He shifted his attention to Gemma. "Ella is my wife. She's a lawyer. You'll like her." He smiled.

Gemma nodded. She didn't want to meet Ella or anyone else for that matter. Not yet.

"Thank you," Damon said. "We'll talk about that, too."

Robert stood, and Gemma clasped onto Damon again, not wanting him to leave her.

"I'll see myself out," Robert said. "Call me."

"I will. Thanks again for everything."

Gemma held her breath until the front door closed with a resounding snick. Finally, she breathed out heavily and tipped her head back. "Are you going to spank me now?"

CHAPTER ELEVEN

Damon chuckled as he looked down at her. "Is that all you've been thinking about for the last fifteen minutes?"

Her cheeks heated, but she nodded. "Yes, Sir." Lying wasn't in her repertoire. "Also, I was wondering when he would leave."

Damon chuckled again and then sobered. "I love your honesty. I want you to do two things, and then I'll spank you."

"You want me to do two things?" She stared at him in confusion.

"Yep. I want you to tell me what was going through your pretty head while you were panicking, and then I want you to sit down at the computer and order some clothes. Can you do those two things?"

She lowered her gaze. "I guess." The whine shocked her and made her flinch.

His chest rumbled as he laughed again. "Sassy girl."

"Maybe that can be a rule, too?" she suggested, playing with the front of his shirt. "I shouldn't sass you."

His laughter increased. She enjoyed the sound and decided

she wanted to hear it more often. She didn't remember him laughing when he was working for her father. But then, her father hadn't been a humorous guy and hadn't liked his employees to be slackers either.

"Maybe you should make the rules instead of me," he suggested.

She lifted her gaze to him, blinking. Was he making a joke?

He grinned and tapped her nose. "I'm teasing. Your list would probably include all sorts of things you enjoy doing in order to get spanked."

Her cheeks heated, and she squirmed on his lap. "I liked it when you spanked me," she mumbled.

"I know you did, baby. And I'll do it every day if it helps you release some of the stress you're carrying. Now, stop avoiding my question. Tell me what you were feeling when Robert arrived."

She lowered her gaze again, not to be defiant but because it was hard to focus when he held her gaze so intently. She took a breath. "I panicked. I was suddenly your slave, Marigold, not Gemma."

He stroked her hair. "I saw that. Why, baby?"

She drew in a deep breath. "My head is all confused. You're supposed to be my Master. I'm your slave. That's what I was prepared for last night—to become someone's slave. My job is to obey you...and that includes servicing your friends."

He flinched and slowly pulled her in closer. He set his forehead against hers. "You will never service my friends." He shuddered as if the idea were abhorrent, which made her muscles loosen. "I will never expose you to them in an intimate way. Do you understand?"

"Yes," she whispered. "Mostly."

He leaned back a few inches. "Look at me, Gemma."

She did as he asked.

"Never. In another dimension, maybe you could have been my submissive and gone to the club with me, and maybe, I would've exposed you in front of people, but not now. Not after this. Not knowing what I know." He shook his head vehemently.

She swallowed. "You keep telling me you're a Dominant. What does that mean?"

He played with a lock of her hair, staring at it, though probably not seeing it. "It's complicated. I'll explain better later, but basically, it means I enjoy role-playing with someone who is submissive. Someone who willingly turns her power over to me and lets me make decisions for her." He narrowed his gaze. "The key word is willingly. Not a slave. Someone who enjoys being controlled for an hour or two or sometimes longer."

"Oh." She wasn't sure she fully understood. "Am I submissive?"

He sighed. "Maybe. I used to fantasize that you might submit to me. You've certainly submitted to me since you got here, but it's hard to say if that would've come naturally to you or if you're confused from years of abuse."

"I like it when you tell me what to do."

"I know, baby, but I don't know the reasons behind it. Don't worry about it right now. We can discuss it much later, okay?"

"Yes, Sir."

He smirked. "See, I can't tell if you call me Sir because it's ingrained in you and you're in Marigold's skin when you do it, or if it would have come naturally had you never been abducted."

"I... I don't know."

"And we aren't going to worry about it today."

"Okay." She had a million questions, but he was right. That wasn't high on the priority list.

"Let's order you some clothes, yeah?" He lifted her and set her on her feet in front of him, tossing the blanket onto the couch before standing and taking her hand. "My computer is in my office."

Gemma was in awe when she stepped into Damon's office. His house had a lot of surprises. She'd expected his office to be a dark room with wood paneling and leather seats at a giant mahogany desk—much like her father's. Instead, it was modern, with a glass-topped desk, white walls, and white leather furniture. The items on the desk were silver—the computer, paper tray, and pencil holder.

It was void of debris. Not a paper out of place. Tall white filing cabinets behind him must have held everything.

Damon led her to a comfortable white leather chair. He lowered into it and pulled her between his legs before lifting her to sit on one of his thighs. Holding her waist, he asked. "Is this okay?"

She wrapped her arms around his neck. "Perfect."

He opened the laptop, clicked several different tabs, and finally opened a site filled with women's clothing. He pulled his hand back from the mouse. "You used to order things from this store. I thought you might like to start here."

She stared at him. Shocked. "You knew where I ordered my clothes?"

"I knew everything, baby." He kissed her cheek.

It was hard for her to wrap her head around that information. She'd been gaga over him like a teenager, but she'd never had any idea he'd felt anything for her.

Her hands were shaking as she moved the mouse around. It was too overwhelming. She released it and turned to him. "Can you pick for me?"

He wrapped his arm around her, keeping her close as he set his chin on her shoulder. "How about if I point out some options."

"Okay."

He started with dresses. "Do you still like to wear skirts and dresses?"

She stared at the screen and blinked several times. "I don't know." She turned to him. "I can't do this."

"Do what? Shop?" He smiled.

"I don't know about clothes, Damon. I don't need them. Can't I just wear your T-shirts?"

"Not forever, baby. Eventually, you'll need to leave the house or guests will come over. You'll want clothes. I'll want you to have clothes. I can't just tuck you into the corner of the couch every time someone arrives."

She shook her head. "I don't like them touching my skin."

"You'll get better. I promise."

Will I? "What if I don't? What if I never get better? What if I'm too much trouble, and you get tired of me clinging to you?"

He lifted her hand to his lips and kissed it. "I'll never get tired of you in a million years."

"I'm needy and scared and nervous and messed up." She sucked back a sob.

"I'm so fucking glad to have you back that I'll dedicate my entire life to helping you get better if that's what it takes, Gemma."

"I panic when you aren't touching me," she countered, feeling the panic rise even now that he *was* touching her.

"Then don't stop touching me," he whispered, rubbing her knuckles against his cheek. "Having you touch me is not a hardship," he teased.

She sighed. "Just choose for me, please."

"Okay."

She relaxed as he moved the mouse around and started putting things in the cart. She didn't care what they were. Right now, clothes held no meaning to her.

After he added all kinds of outfits ranging from casual to dressier, he clicked on lingerie. "You are about the same size as you were before, so I assume you're about a size four. That's what I chose. Small panties, probably. Do you remember your bra size?"

She bit her lip before turning to face him and releasing it. "I remember not wearing a bra very often because I was naïve, young, and stupid and wanted you to notice my breasts."

He gave her a crooked smile. "Oh, baby, I'm well aware of that fact."

She flushed. "You knew that, too?"

"Of course. I told you I paid attention to everything." He nodded at the screen. "Since you aren't sure and you don't have an opinion, I'm going to pick out bras and panties that I like in several sizes. When we figure it out, we'll send the rest back and order more. How's that?"

She hugged his neck and set her head on his shoulder as an answer.

Finally, he was done, and she was relieved. Ordering clothes was too much pressure. He patted her thigh. "Let's see... What was next on our list?"

She couldn't tell if he was teasing, but she responded, "You were going to spank me, *Sir*." She intentionally didn't look at him, and she emphasized the word *Sir* as if she were the sassiest woman on earth.

He chuckled and stood, holding her in his arms. "Wrap your arms and legs around me, naughty girl."

She smiled as she did as he instructed, feeling victorious. She didn't really care if she was weird. She wanted him to spank her again. Maybe he would give her another orgasm as well.

She was hopeful when he carried her to his bedroom and deposited her with a bounce on the bed. He was still standing, but he leaned over her, his hands planted on the mattress alongside her shoulders.

His gaze was intense. "I can't believe you're here. I've been pacing around for two weeks since I saw your picture. At first, I didn't believe it. I wasn't sure it was you. I doubted myself. I'd looked for you everywhere. I'd scanned through thousands of pictures of women trying to find you. And there you were."

She pursed her lips. It must have been hard on him, looking for her. She'd never known. Her father and all of his staff had been murdered, so she'd assumed she'd been alone in the world and no one would ever notice her missing.

She'd prayed and dreamed and pretended that Damon was looking for her, but she'd never really believed that, and she'd stopped hoping two years ago. It had been a fool's dream.

"I haven't slept well in three years," he murmured. "And almost no sleep in the past two weeks. I don't want to now either because I'm afraid I'll wake up, and it will all be a dream."

That's exactly how she felt; she'd told him as much.

"Gemma."

She parted her lips. "Yes?"

"I have no idea if I should be spanking you or touching you or keeping you in my house. I'm scared that I'm making things worse. You need more help than I can give you. I'm not a psychologist."

She shook her head and grabbed his waist. "Please let me stay," she begged. "Please don't send me away." She'd heard him talking about a hospital and a psych ward. "You said it wouldn't be safe," she reminded him, grasping at straws. Anything.

He slid his hands in to cup her face, dropping to his elbows. "I'm not going to take you anywhere, baby."

"Okay." She nodded, breathing heavily. He was scaring her.

"But spanking you? Touching you?" He dropped his forehead to her chest and took deep breaths. "It feels wrong."

"It feels right to me." She was trembling now. Was he going to deny her? "Please, Damon..." Her voice shook. "You said if I answered your questions and let you buy me clothes..."

He lifted his head and met her gaze. "I know. Are you sure you want me to spank you, baby?"

She nodded, her face heating.

"I'm worried about your ability to consent."

"I'm asking you to spank me, Damon. It feels...good. Like I'm alive. Like you're pushing Gemma to the surface or something. Maybe Gemma would have liked to be spanked by you." There was no maybe.

Gemma might not have known anything specific about dominance and submission before she'd been abducted, but she'd known she would have done anything Damon asked. If he'd wanted her to be submissive... If he'd wanted to spank her... She would have eagerly consented. She'd trusted him then, and she trusted him now.

Gemma had dreamed about Damon touching her. Every inch of her skin. With his intense gaze and his hands. She'd wondered what it would have felt like if he'd held her legs open and licked her pussy.

She hadn't been as naïve as he might have believed. Sure, she'd been a virgin, and still was, but her girlfriends who'd come over often had shown her porn and brought her naughty books. They'd joked that since she'd lived in a nunnery, she'd needed to be corrupted somehow.

She'd been enlightened. She'd watched women getting spanked on the internet. Once she'd learned about porn, she'd often opened an incognito window on her computer and watched anything she could find. It had made her squirm. And she'd always thought about Damon doing those things to her.

She found some courage. "Gemma *did* want to be spanked. She thought about it often. She masturbated to visions of you spanking her. And it turns out, she's me. And I still want that from you."

"Okay," he agreed softly. "Turn over." He pushed off the bed so he was standing. "Hands and knees. Face the headboard."

She was salivating at the thought that he was finally going to spank her this morning. She'd craved it from the moment she'd woken up hours ago.

The T-shirt hung loose around her, and Damon pushed it slowly up her body until it gathered across her shoulder blades before he put his palm on her butt. "Drop to your elbows, baby. Bottom in the air."

She turned her head toward him and leaned her cheek on the mattress so she could watch him. It helped her remember where she was and who she was with. Though it wasn't difficult when he was touching her, rubbing her butt cheeks.

Damon wasn't Master J or any of his trainers. Damon's touch was completely different, and it was a treat to be permitted to watch his face.

He smiled at her. "That's a good girl. Keep your eyes on me while I spank you, Gemma. I want you to know who's touching you when you're with me."

She never wanted to be with anyone else again in her life, but she didn't say that aloud.

He set a hand on the small of her back while the other rubbed her cheeks.

Her breath hitched. Nothing about this experience resembled anything she'd experienced in three years. Damon wasn't angry. He was completely calm. He wasn't doing anything against her will. His touch was sensual. Already, she craved more. She wanted him to reach between her legs.

"Why am I spanking you, Gemma?"

She met his gaze. "Because I asked you to?"

He chuckled. "That sounds about right."

She loved the wrinkles at the corners of his eyes when he laughed and the way he stared at her, smiling as if he'd won the lottery. People had stared at her for three years. Her naked body had been exposed to countless people while she'd been forced to perform for them, but she had never been permitted to look them in the eye or even lift her gaze to their faces.

She had been kind of grateful for that command because it had kept her from seeing their leering looks. She'd heard the vileness in their voices, but she hadn't had to put faces to the strangers who had come to torment her.

She winced as she let those thoughts into her consciousness.

"Gemma... What are you thinking about?" Damon's voice was kind, and he continued to rub her skin, up and down the backs of her thighs and all over her ass.

She shook the gross thoughts from her mind. "I'm sorry, Sir." She wanted to be present with Damon, not some asshole she didn't know.

"Tell me. Get it out. Eventually, you need to tell me everything, baby. It's the only way you'll be able to purge it. Tell me what you were thinking."

Her voice was small when she spoke, and it was hard to share, but she couldn't ignore Damon's request. "I like watching your face and how you look at me."

"I'm glad, baby. That's why I insist upon it, but what made you cringe?"

She licked her lips. "I'm glad I never looked at any of Master J's guests. I wasn't permitted to, and I'm glad."

"I'm glad too, baby," Damon said softly. "Did they touch you?"

"Yes," she barely whispered, squeezing her eyes closed at the memory.

"You may keep your eyes closed while you talk, but tell me how they touched you, Gemma." There was an underlying command in Damon's voice that she couldn't ignore. She didn't want to. It wasn't like an order from Master J. Damon's commands didn't precede a punishment. He wouldn't discipline her cruelly for failing.

"Master J would make us stand in the inspection position when he had guests," she whispered, trying to find the courage to tell Damon what she'd been through.

Damon's hands kept stroking her, but his breathing was heavier. "Keep going. Describe it to me, and then I'll chase it all away with a hard spanking before I give you an orgasm."

She shivered. She wanted that.

She took a breath and went back into her head. She was Marigold. She was standing in Master J's library, surrounded by men in suits. The memory was hard to face, and she found herself stepping out of Marigold's body to watch so she could describe the scene as if she were a spectator.

For several long seconds, she surveyed the room. A dozen men, maybe. It was a scene she'd participated in so many times that they all blended together as one. Well-dressed older men in dark suits. Fancy shoes. She had no faces, but she thought they were mostly in their sixties based on their movements and sizes. Many had beer guts.

"Gemma..." Damon encouraged gently.

She flinched and started speaking. "We would stand in his library. Sometimes, just one of us. Sometimes, more. Sometimes, all of us."

"The six of you?" he asked.

"Yes. Six."

"Were there others? Did anyone come and go while you were there?"

She shook her head. "No. I was the first. The others joined over time."

"Okay, what would happen in the library?"

"It's like he had parties or something. There was a bar. Most of the men had drinks in their hands all night."

Damon nudged Gemma's knees out and helped her lie flat on the bed. "Keep going. I want you to be comfortable while you talk." He set his hand on her and ran it all the way up her body. "Do you like me touching you, baby?"

She nodded. "Yes, Sir. Please don't stop. It reminds me where I am and who I'm with."

"Good girl. I want you to focus on my voice when I interrupt to help you remember, okay?"

"Yes, Sir."

"Tell me more."

"Most of the time, we would stand for hours in one spot, feet wide, arms clasped behind us, shoulders back, heads bowed. If we dared lift our gaze, Master J would blindfold us. Often, he blindfolded us anyway." She shuddered. "If we dared violate the rule to keep our eyes on the floor, we would be forced to recite Master J's long list of mantras. A blindfold was much worse than keeping my gaze down because I couldn't see anything at all and wasn't able to anticipate when and where I might be touched."

Damon's hand slid to her shoulders and squeezed. "How did they touch you? Whoever Master J is, he advertises that his slaves are untouched virgins."

She nodded against the mattress. "He's devious. One of the ways he enjoys humiliating his slaves is by proving he can get them aroused and keep them aroused without ever giving them relief."

Damon made a small sound. She couldn't blame him. She also couldn't look at his face and risk seeing his hard jaw and furrowed, angry brow.

"Master J liked to touch our pussies. He would drag his fingers through our folds and toy with our clits to ensure we were wet." She squeezed her eyes closed, trying not to cry. "I didn't want to be wet, Damon," she whimpered. "It made him laugh. It was humiliating."

"It wasn't your fault, Gemma," he said in a firm voice.

"Everyone in the room would wander by and play with our breasts. Tease our nipples. Sometimes, they gave a sharp pinch. If we made a noise or moved, it would be worse. It was a test of my will to stand still for hours while people fondled me. He wanted to prove to everyone that we were well-trained slaves who knew our place and were obedient to a fault. It wasn't worth it to prove him wrong. Every one of us learned that lesson more often than we'd have liked."

"But no one ever penetrated you? Not even Master J?"

"No. They preferred to stroke our skin all over until we were dripping wet and needy. At the end of the evening, Master J would have us all lie on the floor, hands above our heads, knees spread wide, so everyone could see how wet we were and laugh." She shuddered. The laughter had been the worst part—so degrading.

"If Master J didn't like how wet we were when he checked us throughout the evening, he would press a small bullet vibe to our clit for a few seconds and then remove it."

Damon's hand slid up to the back of her hair. "Jesus," he whispered. "And you never had an orgasm?"

She shook her head. "Daffodil did once," she murmured. "We didn't see her for a week. She never spoke of where she'd been or what had happened to her. None of us dared orgasm. Not ever. We were taught to contain our pleasure and save it for our future owners."

"I think that's enough for now, baby. I'm very proud of you for sharing with me. Can I spank you now and chase away the bad feelings?"

"Yes, Sir."

He lifted her hips. "Pull your knees back up but keep them wide, baby."

She returned to the position he'd had her in earlier, her heart racing with the need to be spanked. She craved it like a drug. She hoped he was right, and the spanking would chase away some of the bad.

CHAPTER TWELVE

"Open your eyes. You will watch me while I spank you."

She blinked at him. "Yes, Sir."

"I'm going to warm you up, and then I'm going to spank you until I think you've had enough, but if we're going to make a habit of this, you need a safeword. Do you know what a safeword is, Gemma?"

She nodded. "I read about them, and Master J always told us that slaves don't get safewords."

"Well, you're not a slave. You're a precious human being with full autonomy. If you're going to submit to me like this, you need to understand that it's always your choice. You have all the power. I can only touch you if you ask me to. I will never force you to do anything. Understood?"

"Yes, Sir," she whispered.

"The universal safeword is *red*. If you say red, I stop immediately. If you say yellow, I slow down and check with you."

"Okay."

"What's your safeword, baby?"

"Red."

"Good girl. You must use it if I spank you too hard or too long or in a spot you don't like. If you don't stop me, I won't be able to trust you."

"Okay."

"I will always start gently and build up the pressure as I warm up your bottom. I'll stop when I think you've had enough."

"Will you..." She swallowed, finding the will to ask for what she wanted. "Will you do it harder than last night?"

"Do you want me to spank you harder?"

"Yes, Sir." She wanted to *feel*. When he'd spanked her last night, she'd felt alive and human for the first time in three years. She wanted to feel that again, but more of it.

"Ready, baby?"

"Yes, Sir." Her legs were trembling from anticipation. She was close to begging.

Finally, he lifted his palm and swatted her. His gaze was on her butt, but he glanced at her every few strokes.

She kept her gaze on his face because he'd ordered her to, and she didn't want to risk him stopping.

After a few swats, he picked up the pace and struck her harder, taking her breath away. In the best way. She gasped and wiggled her butt, wanting more.

He paused and leaned over to stroke a lock of hair from her face. "You okay, baby?"

"Yes, Sir," she panted. It felt amazing. There was no way to explain why she needed this, but she needed it more than air or water. She'd hardly been touched in three years. Isolation and restraint were Master J's favorite forms of punishment. Someone bathed her occasionally, and on the nights when Master J had guests, people stroked her skin until she wanted to scream.

She needed the intensity of this contact. She needed the eye contact Damon demanded. She needed to watch his face while he concentrated on spanking her. She needed to come.

After a few minutes, Gemma's eyes rolled back as the stinging pain became somehow blissful.

Damon stopped and rubbed her skin again.

She whimpered, not wanting him to stop.

His lips came to her temple, and he brushed her hair back. "Eyes on me, Gemma."

Her mouth was dry. "Sir..." Even though he'd insisted she not call him Sir, she couldn't stop it. Sometimes, it felt natural. It rolled from her lips. It felt exactly right while he was dominating her like this.

"Would you like me to stop, baby?"

Her eyes shot wide. "No. Please. More."

"Then stay with me. Watch me."

"Okay," she managed with a slight nod.

His hand went back to her bottom, and he continued, his swats more intense than before and raining down on the backs of her thighs, too. Every time he struck the seam of her butt and her thighs, she gasped. His strokes vibrated her pussy.

That desperate feeling returned, and she prayed he would not deny her the orgasm she sought.

She couldn't keep her eyes on him any longer. When they rolled back, she went into her head and moaned. For once, she wasn't thinking about Master J or his trainers. She laser-focused on Damon and his palm.

Moments later, he stopped, immediately sliding his hand between her legs.

She cried out as his fingers found her clit, lifting her face up and tipping her head back. "Oh, God."

"You're dripping wet, baby," he cooed. "So needy. This is for me, isn't it?"

She nodded and breathed out, "Yes, Sir. It's yours."

He rubbed her clit harder. It felt so fucking good, but it wasn't enough.

She rocked back, trying to get more contact. "I need…"

"What do you need, Gemma?" he demanded.

"I need you inside me." She'd felt this craving before. She'd felt it many times when she'd masturbated to thoughts of Damon while she'd still lived in her father's house. She'd often reach inside her pussy with a few fingers, but she'd never inserted anything larger.

"Not gonna fuck you, Gemma," he said gently, his lips nibbling around her heated ass before he met her gaze again. "Not today. But I'll give you what you need." He circled her clit and then rubbed it hard and fast, his other hand coming to the small of her back to hold her steady.

She realized she'd been rocking, squirming, wiggling. He'd put a stop to that.

"Look at me, Gemma. Eyes on me while you come for me."

She turned her head to the side again, panting, shaking, close to imploding. "Please."

He slid his fingers through her folds. "Have you had anything inside you, baby?"

She nodded. "My fingers… Tampons…"

He stroked through her wetness several times, holding her gaze. His brow was furrowed as if he were trying to make a decision. Finally, he swallowed. "I'm going to push one finger into you, okay?"

She nodded vigorously. "Please, Damon."

He pushed at her entrance and then eased his finger into her.

She whimpered. It was so hard to focus on him. When she felt the base of his hand against her pussy, she knew his finger was buried deep. The heel of his palm was against her clit, and he rubbed it hard.

Gemma's mouth fell open. *Please, please, please…*

She stopped breathing. Her entire body tightened. And then she came. Hard. The sound in the room was probably her screaming as her orgasm took over her entire body. The pulses milked his finger, and she rocked to press against his palm.

Damon didn't remove his hand until she was panting and shaking. She let her knees slide out from under her, leaving her flat on the bed, sated, still trying to pull in oxygen.

The T-shirt was bunched up above her breasts. She didn't care. After a moment, she tugged it off and dropped back down onto her chest.

Damon's hands were all over her, rubbing her back and soothing her heated skin. "So gorgeous," he murmured.

"Mmm," was all she could manage.

Damon leaned over and kissed her neck. "Can I pull a sheet over you, baby?"

She shook her head. "No. Please." She finally found the energy to blink at him. "Join me."

He drew in a breath, hesitating.

She flinched, panic seizing her. Maybe he didn't want to join her. Her lip quivered.

He grabbed the back of her neck when she started to look away. "Eyes on mine, Gemma."

She was fighting another round of tears.

He leaned in closer. "Do not for one moment doubt my feelings for you. If I have my way, you'll be mine for the rest of our lives. My hesitation has nothing to do with wanting you. I'm worried about my self-control right now, Gemma. My dick is so fucking hard, it's going to bust out of my jeans from spanking your fucking sexy body and watching you come for me. I won't take advantage of you while you're so raw and hurting and confused."

She was trembling, but she nodded. "Okay." He sounded sincere.

"You need more sleep, baby. Actually, we both do. Neither of us has slept well in three years." He released her and ran a hand through his hair. "If I climb into this bed with you, will you keep your hands away from my cock?"

"If you want me to, but I'm pretty familiar with it after last night," she pointed out, trying to smile.

He groaned. "It took every ounce of my willpower to let that play out without murdering everyone in the room with my bare hands. The last thing I wanted was for you to suck my cock in front of all those people. You didn't even know who I was, and you weren't given a choice."

"I knew. I mean, as soon as I inhaled your scent, I thought I knew," she reminded him. "It helped a lot. I was so scared as I approached you. And then I smelled your cologne and pretended it was you the entire time. It didn't even matter if it was you or not. All that mattered was that I believed your cock was in my mouth. It made it much better."

"I'm glad, but you're not doing that again for a long time."

"You were so kind." Tears fell. She couldn't stop them as she remembered what he'd done for her. "You let my hair curtain my mouth and blocked over half of your erection with your fist. It gave me the strength to continue. I knew then that whoever you were, you weren't a total asshole."

He reached for her cheek and stroked her skin. "I haven't always been the best human being, but I'll spend the rest of my life doing my best to be everything you need me to be if you'll have me, baby. And I can't do that if I climb into this bed and hold your naked body. I don't have that kind of willpower."

"Why do you need willpower? Why don't you just fuck me and stop trying to hold back?"

"Because you can't consent to something like that. You need time to heal before I push my cock into you."

She rolled to her side and grabbed his hand. "I'll be good. I promise. I just need you to hold me. I can't sleep without you."

His gaze scanned down her body.

It was odd because so many men had seen her naked, gawked at her, and made snide comments. Touched her inappropriately. And yet, Damon was erasing that, chipping away at the humiliation and degradation. He looked at her like she mattered. Like she was important. Like he cared.

His hand slid reverently down her arm. "You are so fucking sexy. Every inch of you. Better than I ever imagined. And I'm sorry that you were treated like an object. I hate that anyone ever saw you naked. I'm grateful that no one raped you, but in a way, they did anyway, with their mind-fucking and their hands."

"I like it when *you* touch me," she murmured.

"I'm glad, but I'm worried I'm doing more harm than good."

"You're not," she insisted. "Please." She knew she was begging, but she didn't want him to leave the room. He looked like he planned to bolt.

Finally, he kicked off his shoes, scooted her toward the center of the bed, and climbed in next to her. He turned her away from him and spooned her from behind, holding her against his fully-clothed body. His hand smoothed down her hair. "Sleep, baby."

"You won't leave me?"

"No. I'll be right here. I promise."

CHAPTER THIRTEEN

Damon held Gemma close. They both needed it. But she couldn't settle. Every time she almost fell asleep, she bolted back awake, gasping and whimpering.

He kept stroking her hair, trying to help her relax, but nothing worked. She would drift off and then start mumbling. Her arms twitched constantly.

"Gemma," he murmured. It hurt him to see her like this. "What can I do, baby?"

She tucked her head against his hand. After a moment, she rolled to her back next to him and lifted her arms over her head. "Restrain me," she whispered.

"What?"

"My wrists. Cuff them away from me. Either pulled out to the sides or above my head."

He swallowed hard. "No, baby." She'd mentioned that was how she'd been sleeping, but he couldn't do that to her. He wouldn't. He didn't want her restrained ever for any reason. Perhaps by his hands when she was awake for her sexual gratification, but no fucking way was he going to strap her down so she could sleep.

She looked much calmer than he felt as she lifted her hand to his face and stroked his cheek. "Please."

"No, Gemma. Don't make me do something like that. No one should ever be cuffed to a bed to sleep. It's inhumane."

"It's how I've slept for three years. Naked and spread open."

He rubbed his eyes, trying to block that image out of his mind and control his fury. The last thing she needed was for him to start screaming in frustration. If she weren't in the room right now, he would punch a hole through the wall and throw everything he could get his hands on.

"Do you have some cuffs?" she asked softly.

He groaned. "Yes, but I'm not using them to tie a sleeping woman to my bed. Ever."

"It's what I need."

"You slept during the night without them. I held you," he pointed out.

"I think I was so far past exhausted that I was comatose."

He glanced around and came up with an idea. It was a horrible idea, but if she really couldn't settle without restraints, maybe it would work. "Don't move." He kissed her lips and then slid from the bed.

After opening his closet, he grabbed his toy bag, tugged it closer, unzipped it, and found what he was looking for.

She smiled when he returned to her, holding up four Velcro cuffs. She was so fucking gorgeous. She continually took his breath away. Her breasts were high and tight and so beautiful he could stare at them for hours. If he couldn't convince her to start wearing clothes, he was going to have to get used to seeing them and not instantly getting hard. As if that could ever happen.

Misunderstanding his intentions, she lifted her arms above her head wide and spread her legs open toward the corners of the bed.

Jesus.

Damon climbed up beside her, dropped the cuffs, and leaned over her. "I'm not fucking restraining you, baby. I'll compromise though. I'll put the cuffs on your wrists and ankles. Perhaps the weight of them will make you feel restrained."

She sighed. "I don't know…"

"It's my only offer."

She bit her lower lip. "What if I can't sleep?"

"Then we'll get you some melatonin or something." He stared at her, waiting. "Take it or leave it."

"Okay."

When she didn't lower her arms, he reached up to cuff them and let her leave them above her head. He hated that she actually spread her legs wider. He had no intention of letting her sleep in this position. The cuffs he might be able to stomach, but not this spread-position. Besides, he wanted to hold her, and he wouldn't be able to with her limbs stretched out in an X.

Nevertheless, he climbed between her legs to cuff first one ankle and then the other before setting his hands on her knees and lifting his gaze. He wanted to shift his eyes up to hers, but instead, his gaze lingered as he soaked in her body.

Her pussy was so smooth and naked. He didn't ask her why or more importantly how. He would save that question for another time.

Suddenly, he caught the edge of something red on her inner thigh and leaned closer as he remembered it would be the tattoo her abductor had marked her with.

It looked familiar… "Jesus, fuck," he blurted as he grabbed her leg too roughly and pushed her knee higher and wider so he could see her inner thigh better.

"What?"

Damon blinked several times. He couldn't catch his breath. He was seeing things. Imagining this. It couldn't be real.

"Damon? You're scaring me," she whispered.

He slid his hand up her inner thigh from her knee to the tattoo. "I'm sorry, baby. Who did this?"

She flinched but said nothing.

"Gemma?" He lifted his gaze to hers.

She frowned at him.

"Who did it, baby?" he demanded.

She glared at him. "Do you think we took a field trip to a tattoo parlor called Roses Are Us, and we all sat around with the general public waiting our turn to have someone fucking mark our skin against our will?" Her words were venomous and filled with anger.

He released her thigh immediately and sat back on his heels. Shit. She was right.

She shoved back a foot and sat up, pulling her knees up to her chest and wrapping her arms around them, her face tipped toward the mattress as she started rocking.

Damon took several deep breaths. "I'm so sorry."

She jerked her gaze up. "For what, Damon?" Her voice was higher pitched and laced with malice. "For snapping at me because I can't tell you the name of the tattoo artist who pulled a ski mask over my head, strapped my naked body down to a table, and fucking inked the inside of my thigh while I screamed past the bit between my teeth?"

Bile rose in Damon's throat at the visual. He couldn't move or breathe.

She dropped her knees and glared at him, rightfully so. "You keep saying you want me to tell you every detail about my captivity, but are you sure you can stand to hear about it? It's ugly. I don't have fun tales of slumber parties with the girls. I don't even know any of their fucking names," she shouted.

Damon stayed still. He deserved her wrath, and he wanted her to get out whatever she needed any time she needed without interruption. Because she was right. He'd insisted she tell him. He needed to be man enough to listen and absorb some of her pain.

"You want to know who gave me this tattoo?" she shouted sarcastically. "Here's what I know. I'm pretty sure it was four men who held me down to the fucking wooden table. My arms were cuffed to the legs on one end, and one of my ankles was cuffed to the far corner. A thick strap extended across my hips. Several hands held my upper body, their fingers all over my tits. Several other hands held my free leg high and wide so that my pussy was wide open. They spent the entire time commenting on how pretty it was and tapping my clit occasionally just to torment me."

Damon thought he was going to be sick.

"It took over an hour for that fucking sadistic prick to ink my inner thigh. I didn't even know what he was doing. No one told me. I just knew it hurt worse than any pain I'd ever experienced in my life. I thought I was going to die. It seemed like they were cutting a giant hole in my leg. I assumed I would bleed out and die on that table." Her voice rose again. "And I prayed for that mercy. I prayed I would fucking die so I wouldn't have to endure another moment of their psychotic games."

She leaned back, shaking violently. "When they were done, my voice was gone from screaming, and those bastards cuffed my other ankle to the corner of the table and left the ski mask on me so I had to spend all night wondering what the fuck they'd done to me. The area burned. I kept screaming, but no sound came out."

Damon was frozen. He didn't know what the fuck to do. Should he reach out and touch her, pull her into his arms, or tell her how sorry he was? Nothing would erase her pain, and he was a fucking bastard for thinking he could handle this on his own.

Finally, she lifted her gaze and met his. Her voice was calmer. "So, if you want to know who did that to me, you're going to have to ask someone else. I have no fucking idea."

"I'm sorry," he whispered. It wasn't sufficient, but glib words would never be enough.

"I know," she murmured, wrapping her arms around herself and shivering. She instantly dropped her arms away from her breasts before seeming to realize it was okay to cover herself now. "I think I'd like a shirt please."

Thank fuck.

Damon slid off the end of the bed and grabbed the shirt she'd removed, returning to pull it over her head. When it was covering her, he sat next to her and gently wrapped an arm around her.

She finally leaned into him, grabbing his forearm, and began to sob.

He pulled her closer, holding her against his side, and kissed the top of her head. Speaking would be senseless right now. She needed to cry. She would need to purge and cry a thousand times, and he needed to fucking stop reacting like some sort of neanderthal each time.

This situation was different though. That was no ordinary tattoo. That was the precise logo for Robert's club, Roses and Thorns.

Damon's head was spinning with questions. Thousands of them. He would need to call Robert and tell him, but that wasn't his top priority right now. First, he needed to comfort Gemma and find a way to help her sleep.

They *both* needed sleep.

After holding her at his side until her heart rate slowed down and she stopped violently shaking, he eased her onto her back. He leaned over her, stroked her cheek, and then kissed her forehead. Words weren't sufficient. He was going to have to show her how much he cared and stop acting like a raving lunatic every time she shared something.

He *did* want her to tell him everything. If he kept reacting so harshly, she would stop talking.

The lighting in the room wasn't ideal. The sun was bright outside and illuminating the room as if all the lights were on. "Would you like me to close the blinds?" he murmured.

She shook her head. "No."

He lifted her arms gently over her head, watching her face closely. When she blew out a relaxed breath, he slid down alongside her and let his arm drape over the top of her wrists. He nudged her legs apart with his knee and settled his leg between hers.

He kissed her temple. "That's as much restraint as I can stomach, baby. It will have to work."

She took a deep breath and let it out. "Okay." She squirmed a bit, trying to get comfortable.

He couldn't imagine how anyone could sleep with their limbs restrained. It was unfathomable. But if that was the only option for three years, he supposed eventually someone might get used to it.

"I'm sorry," he whispered against her cheek.

"I know," she responded just as softly.

He was sorry for so many things. Those two words were loaded. He was sorry for freaking out, sorry for yelling, sorry for demanding answers she didn't have. But mostly, he was sorry anything like that had happened to her.

Every time she added to the saga, his driving need to obliterate her abductor from the face of the earth increased. Him and every single person who worked for him.

Eventually, he would do it. Somehow, he would figure out

who that pond scum was and teach him a lesson. A slow agonizing death would be too light of a sentence, but it was the only thing Damon would have at his disposal.

He gritted his jaw as he imagined restraining that fucker and cutting off one finger or toe a day. Then he'd stab his eyes out on day five so the bastard couldn't see what might happen next. The man should be naked and have his cock fondled constantly so that it stayed hard for a month without release. Or how about three years?

The ideas were endless, and Damon could feel his humanity leaving him. He was going to need to rein in his thoughts. If he murdered twenty people in their sleep for their part in Gemma's suffering, he would end up in jail, and that wouldn't help her out at all.

Perhaps he was filled with wishful thinking, but he was starting to let himself believe she needed him. Not just needed but maybe she could even love him. He hadn't permitted himself to think that far into the future about what might happen if he ever found her. He hadn't let himself hope she could be his. Instead, he'd concentrated on the important part —rescuing her. Setting her free.

It might be time to call Jagger. Damon hadn't been willing to involve the FBI in his plans before he'd gotten Gemma to safety, but now that he had her, perhaps he should let the FBI get involved.

That plan could backfire on him, too. Just like going to the cops. Anything that drew attention to him could be detrimental to Gemma. But finding the seller could prove difficult if he didn't have the help of the FBI.

Gemma twitched, and he glanced at her before applying slight pressure to her wrists. She settled a few seconds later. Her shallow breathing indicated she was finally resting.

He needed to sleep when she slept, so he closed his eyes

and forced his mind to stop running rampant. The deeply seeded desperation to find Master J was powerful, but right now, his focus needed to be on helping her heal.

It felt like only moments went by before Damon jolted back awake. Gemma was moaning in her sleep. The sound wasn't from distress or pain. It was erotic.

He stared at her, wondering what she was dreaming. Her lips were parted, and her head was tipped back. Lastly, he realized she was grinding her pussy against his thigh. Perhaps pressing his knee between her legs hadn't been the best plan.

Damon set his palm on her pelvis to steady her as he eased his leg away from her pussy. Jesus, she was wet, and so were his jeans.

Luckily, she seemed to settle, her breathing returning to normal over the next few minutes.

Damon's breath did not, and his cock was fucking hard against her thigh. Having sex with her was out of the question. He was breathing heavily against her biceps.

"Damon..." she moaned.

Shit.

"Please..."

She made it very difficult to turn her down. She was insatiable, and he couldn't blame her, but he felt like a fucking asshole touching her, taking from her. *Giving to her,* he reminded himself. Giving her what she wanted. Giving her what she deserved after what she'd been through.

He lifted his head and found her staring at him, eyes glazed, chest heaving, legs moving restlessly once again. "Make love to me. Chase it away."

He released her arms, and she brought them down around his neck, hugging him. He reached for the Velcro at her wrists and removed the damn cuffs. He hated seeing her in them. "You were dreaming," he murmured against her shoulder before reaching down to remove the restraints from her ankles next.

"Mmm-hmmm. Now, take your pants off."

He closed his eyes and held his breath. *Don't do it.*

She lowered her arm from his neck and flattened her fingers on top of his hand at her pelvis. She pushed his hand lower, over the edge of the T-shirt, until her wet heat was on his palm.

"Okay, baby," he whispered. He was not going to fuck her, but he would give her the release she craved. Again. *Jesus.*

She moaned when he stroked through her folds, her fingers pressing against his as if she needed more pressure. Her head tipped back, and she arched her chest, her hard nipples visible against the cotton shirt.

He needed to taste her. Not just taste. He needed to consume her. Sliding down the bed, he positioned himself between her legs. "Push your shirt up and play with your nipples, baby."

She arched her chest higher and groaned. Her hands were fisted at her sides. "I...can't."

"You can." She needed to learn to touch herself. She needed to know that she could. It was totally out of his wheelhouse to let a submissive touch herself. Normally, he would insist otherwise. The few times he'd been in a relationship with a sub, he'd ordered her to keep her hands to herself and save her orgasms for him. He'd been known to talk dirty to them on the phone while insisting they keep their fingers away from their pussy.

That was not going to happen with Gemma. "Slide your shirt up, Gemma," he ordered. He felt like he was walking on a thin tightrope. She seemed to crave the commands, but he hated dominating her so blatantly. Hated thinking he might be causing more harm than good.

She whimpered as she obeyed, and God, her tits were

amazing. So perfect. Round and high and sexy as hell. Her rosy nipples were small and tight, the areolas less than an inch wide.

"Cup your tits. Thumb your nipples," he demanded.

She was shaking as she slid her hands up her belly toward her breasts, and then she was holding them, obeying his order, flicking her nipples, making them grow into tighter little beads.

"Pinch them, baby." His voice was gravelly, and he had to press his cock against the mattress. He nearly came when she pinched those sweet buds between her fingers and thumbs. "Good girl." His voice cracked.

He slid his hands up her inner thighs, urging them wider, his gaze on her soaking wet pussy. Her folds were so pretty. Pink and swollen. Her clit was pushing out of the hood, pulsing, demanding.

When he lowered his face to suck her pussy, his mouth wide to encompass as much of her as possible, she nearly shot off the bed.

"*Damon*," she cried out.

He moaned against her pussy, knowing the vibrations would drive her crazy. A glance upward told him she was still fingering her nipples, pinching and pulling on them. *Good girl.*

He inhaled her scent as deeply as possible, memorizing her, heart racing, cock in revolt. He was going to come, but she didn't need to know it. Finally, he gave up fighting the orgasm and ground his erection into the mattress against his jeans.

He was suddenly starving for her and thrust his tongue into her tight channel before flicking it over her clit.

She made the sexiest noises, squirming around so much that he had to steady her with his hands on her thighs. It worked out fine because he kept his thumb over the majority of the tattoo so he didn't have to see it and remind himself of what she'd been subjected to.

"*Damon*," she screamed.

Her body stiffened a moment before she started writhing, pulsing, throbbing.

He suckled her clit, not easing off until she flinched.

Damn, she was gorgeous when she came.

CHAPTER FOURTEEN

Damon watched as she slowly relaxed into the mattress, breathing heavily. Her hand slid down her body and covered his, pushing against him. "Hurts," she murmured.

He lifted his head up to look at her, fear freaking him out. "What hurts, baby?" He released her thighs and wiped his mouth on the back of his hand.

She blew out a breath when he let her go. "The tattoo."

He tipped his head down to look at it, relieved that he hadn't hurt her himself. It hurt though? He framed it with his hands, holding her leg steady, examining it.

It was indeed the exact rose and thorn design Robert used for his club logo. It couldn't be a coincidence. Robert's logo had been created by a private artist, but Robert owned the trademark. Damon was certain of that. The two of them had discussed it when Damon had first joined the club ten years ago.

Damon grazed a thumb gently over the tattoo. It looked perfectly healed. The skin was slightly raised as expected. It wasn't infected. "What hurts, baby?"

"Inside," she whimpered, "When you push on it."

He frowned, not wanting to hurt her but needing to understand. "How long have you had it?"

"I don't know. A month maybe?"

"I'm going to put some pressure on it in a few places. Tell me where it hurts, okay?"

"Yes."

He used his index finger to apply slight pressure in a circle around it, gradually making the circle smaller until she winced. "There," she said.

Damon stiffened. Was there something under the skin? He didn't want her to suffer any longer, so he stopped prodding, but he wanted someone else to look at it. Immediately. *Shit. And fuck.*

He also needed to contact Robert because it was not a coincidence that this fucking tattoo was his logo.

Damon rose onto his elbows. "I need you to be brave for me, Gemma."

"Okay." She shuddered, not questioning him.

"I need to take a few pictures of this tattoo."

She winced.

"I'll aim the camera so close that no one can even tell what part of the body it is, okay?"

She nodded, chewing on her bottom lip.

"Unfortunately, I also want someone to look at it."

She nodded, her face draining of color.

Dammit.

"I'm going to make a few calls," he told her as he climbed up her body. He pulled her shirt over her chest and down to cover her pussy. He'd need to find something else for her to put on to better cover her. She needed panties. Today. Not tomorrow.

Reaching across her, he grabbed his cell phone from the nightstand and made his first call to Robert.

Robert picked up instantly. "Hey. How is she?"

146

"Better." Damon leaned on one hip alongside her, keeping an eye on her as she stared at him. "I need you to see something. Can you come over?"

"Of course. Be there in ten."

"Can you perhaps bring Ella and maybe stop for some panties?"

Gemma pursed her lips.

"Will do. Anything in particular?"

"Something modest."

"Okay, see you in thirty."

"Robert and Ella are coming over?" she asked in a shaky voice.

"Yes." There was no way to sugarcoat the problem, and Damon didn't want to keep anything from Gemma. "That tattoo is the logo for Robert's club."

Gemma swallowed. "Could it just be similar?"

"No. It's exact. And he had an artist sketch it. There's a connection." *And I hate it.* He kissed her quickly and then placed his next call.

Jagger answered, thank God. "What's up?"

"Jagger. Need your help."

"Okay. I never like it when you start a conversation like that." He chuckled.

"This is important. And you're not going to like it. And I need it to be off the record. Plus...bring an ELF Field Meter."

"Jesus, Damon. Is that all?" he asked sarcastically.

"Yes. When can you get here?"

"I'm going to have to swing by my office to get the meter. Give me an hour."

"Okay. Don't tell anyone."

Jagger sighed. "I'm not going to like this at all, am I?"

"No." Damon ended the call.

"What's a Field Meter?" Gemma asked.

"It's like a metal detector."

"For what?"

He pulled her closer and stroked a lock of hair off her forehead. "I need you to trust me, baby. Okay?"

She gave a slight nod.

"Technically, you hardly know me. I know I'm asking for a lot, but I want you to be safe and whole and happy. Those are my goals. Jagger and Robert are my closest friends. I've known Robert most of my life, even though he's ten years older than me. Our fathers were friends. They were murdered a week apart."

Gemma flinched.

Damon gave her a squeeze and continued. "It was a long time ago. No need to fret."

"Oh."

"Anyway. Robert and I became close. Though our fathers undoubtedly lived a bit under the law, they weren't murderers or kidnappers."

"Like my father..." she mused softly. "He wasn't a good man either, was he?"

Damon held her gaze. "He was no different from my father. He did some things that weren't particularly legal, but he didn't have people killed or kidnapped."

She nodded, though he wasn't sure if she believed him. At twenty, she had undoubtedly done her best to ignore her father's business activities, but she hadn't been ignorant. "He did things that weren't legal, didn't he?"

Damon shrugged. "Like I said, he didn't kidnap or kill anyone. Laundering money isn't a crime I would put in that same category."

"Why did Master J have him killed?" She played with the hem of her shirt, staring at her lap.

"I don't know," Damon answered honestly. "I've always thought money was involved. I suspect your father owed someone money."

"Master J?"

"Maybe. That does seem likely since it's a bit too convenient that he would have had your father and his staff killed and then abducted you."

She stiffened. "You think I was collateral damage?"

Damon sighed. "I'm not sure."

She nodded slowly. "Master J wasn't there the day of the attack. I mean, I don't think so. I was drugged and taken to him. I woke up in his dungeon."

Damon gritted his teeth. He wanted to know more about this dungeon, but now wasn't a good time. Every time he got her to talk, she ended up exhausted, and people were coming over any minute.

"I know you have dozens of questions about your father, and I think it would be better to wait and discuss that topic when you're stronger, okay?"

"Yes."

"Back to Robert. As I said, he owns a fetish club. Four of them, actually. But the main branch is here in Denver. I'm a member. I've been a member for ten years." He toyed with a lock of her hair while he spoke.

He couldn't stop touching her. Any part of her. Even if it was just her hair. He'd hardly ever dared to touch her three years ago while he'd worked under her father's roof, had rarely made eye contact with her, and had spoken no more than a few sentences to her.

He kept blinking, reminding himself she was really here. No one was alive who could stop him from touching her or punish either of them for expressing how they felt.

"The other man coming is Jagger. We met in college, and we've been friends ever since. I would trust either of them with my life, and more importantly, I would trust them with yours."

She nodded again. "Okay."

He gave her a quick kiss. It was so...familiar, as if they were a couple and had been for years. He'd had her only a handful of hours and already he felt a strong possessiveness. He wanted the right to kiss her anytime. He was claiming that right.

Cupping her face, he spoke again. "May I please take a few pictures? I want Robert to see the tattoo, but I don't want him to have to stare at your inner thigh."

"Okay."

Damon sat up and gently lifted her knee up and out. He tucked the T-shirt over her pussy, completely covering her. Not that he intended to get even an inch of her private parts in the photo, but he knew it would make her feel better.

"Hold still for me, baby," he whispered as he lined the camera up and zoomed in on the tattoo. He took three quick shots.

Gemma flinched each time.

Damon lowered the camera. "Did he take pictures of you?"

She sucked in a breath but didn't answer him as she pulled her leg back down and squeezed her thighs together.

Damon felt his temper rising. He took a deep breath and slid off the bed. She'd asked him to stop reacting so violently, and he was failing her already. If that motherfucker took pictures, what did he do with them?

Gemma slowly sat and scooted to the edge of the mattress. "I think he enjoyed the humiliation more than anything else."

Damon rolled his shoulders. He reminded himself that he'd known the man took pictures of her. That's how Damon had found her and was able to bid on her. But how many had he taken? How often? What was he doing with them now?

She tipped her head back. She was shaking again. "That's a lot of people."

He knew she was referring to his friends. He squatted in

front of her, his hands on the bed on either side of her. "If you panic, I'll ask them to leave as quickly as possible."

She swiped at a tear. "I don't want to be so messed up."

He scooted closer. "I know, baby. Give yourself a break though. You're under a lot of stress. No one expects anything from you. They understand."

She looked away, though he didn't think she was seeing anything. Just staring into space.

"Talk to me. Tell me what you're thinking. Feeling."

After a long pause, she spoke. "It's like there's two of me, and it's very scary."

"That makes sense. You've been through an unimaginably horrible experience. It's your mind's way of coping. I could practically see the moment Gemma went into hiding and your brain switched to an automatic slave mode earlier." His voice was calm and reverent, and he stroked her arm while he spoke.

She nodded. "Marigold. She's me. She's a slave. She controls me sometimes. I can't stop her. She's on autopilot. She thinks she's right." Gemma lifted her gaze. "That sounds crazy."

"No." He shook his head. "Not at all. I bet you had to tuck Gemma away and hide her for a long time. To protect her. It was very brave of you, and I'm so glad you hid her and saved her so she would still be there when I found you."

She seemed to consider his words. "Yes. That's exactly what happened. There was one day a few months after I was kidnapped... I was in that kennel for so many hours my legs went numb. I was angry. Furious. I had been argumentative every chance I got, and every time, I was punished for my insolence. He was trying to break me. And I knew he was succeeding. I was losing myself. And..."

She drew in a deep breath, hesitating. "I realized two things. I would go mad if I spent much more time in that kennel, and I didn't want to lose Gemma forever. So, I hid her and pretended to be Marigold."

When she glanced at Damon, he smiled. "That was very brave, and I'm so proud of you."

"I don't know if it was the right decision. I hated giving in and letting Master J control my every move. It meant he'd finally broken me, and I became a shell of myself. A robot. It scared me to death, and I have no idea if I made the right decision. Maybe I should've fought harder, longer, forced myself to endure the kennel every day if it meant holding on to my humanity."

Damon shook his head. "You did the right thing, baby. You preserved yourself. You saved Gemma, and I'm so damn grateful. I'm not sure what I would've done if I hadn't been able to reach you. I would've been devastated. I've never been more relieved in my life than I was when you looked me in the eye and recognized me last night."

She wrapped her arms around him. "Me, too."

CHAPTER FIFTEEN

The doorbell rang, and Damon gripped Gemma's thighs as he rose. He was still reeling from learning she'd occasionally been kept in a kennel. Plus, she'd spoken of it so matter-of-factly.

Pulling his shit together for the millionth time, he tipped her head back, kissed her, and checked her pulse. "Stay here, okay. I'll be right back."

She grabbed his hand and held on to him. Finally, she nodded and released him. "Okay."

"Two minutes."

He hated leaving her there, but he didn't want her to freak out downstairs either. He took the stairs two at a time and jogged to the front door. When he opened it, he found Robert and Ella, just as expected. It wasn't as if a stranger could show up at his door. They would need to either know the gate code or call him to open it.

Damon pulled the door open wider. "Thank you for coming."

Ella held up a shopping bag, smiling. "I brought girl things." She came closer and wrapped her free arm around

Damon, hugging him. She had always been sweet, kind, and sensitive. "I can't believe you found her. I'm so glad. Is she okay?"

Ella looked past him and scanned the room. "I mean, of course, she's not okay. I just don't know what to say."

He gave her a squeeze. "It's okay. I understand. How about if I take you upstairs to meet her?"

"I'll stay down here," Robert suggested quickly. He was probably still unnerved by how Gemma had reacted to him the first time he'd arrived.

Damon shut the door and pointed toward the kitchen. "Help yourself to a drink. May I suggest something stiff?" Robert was going to lose his fucking mind when he saw the pictures.

Robert lifted both brows. "Damon, you're freaking me out."

Damon simply nodded. A whole lot of freak out was warranted here.

Robert sighed and headed for the kitchen.

Damon turned toward Ella. "I can't begin to predict how she's going to react to meeting you. She's straddling two worlds right now, and lots of things trigger her."

Ella nodded. "I understand. Robert explained. I'm not going to pretend I have a single clue what either of you is going through, but I want you to know I see all kinds of things in my line of work, especially when I take pro bono cases. I've had more women than I can count in my office after being abused in ways that make me cringe."

Before he could comment, she held up a hand. "I'm not suggesting there's any comparison. I've never once had a woman who'd been abducted and held for three years as a slave. But I'm sensitive. That's all I'm saying."

Damon gave her another hug. She was right. She absolutely did have more empathy than many other humans.

He led Ella up the stairs and down the hall, knocking on the master bedroom door before opening it.

He entered slowly with Ella next to him. "Gemma, this is Ella, Robert's wife."

Gemma was biting her bottom lip, staring, still sitting where he'd left her. Finally, she released her lip and gave them a slight smile.

"I brought you some things," Ella said softly, holding up the bag. "I wasn't sure what you might like, so I grabbed a variety."

"Thank you," Gemma said, her shoulders relaxing. Thank God.

"Your hair is so gorgeous," Ella said as she came closer.

Gemma blushed. "Thank you. It's... It needs a cut."

"I'm sure it's been a while. I have an amazing hairdresser I can recommend. She's discreet and understanding, and she'll come to the house if you'd like."

Gemma smiled brighter. "Really?"

"Yes. She was a client of mine."

"Ella's a lawyer," Damon interjected.

Gemma nodded.

"Anyway, I've known Jaycee for years. I handled her messy divorce. She volunteers at a women's shelter, and she's helped me out many, many times when I've had a client who needed to stay out of the public eye."

"Am I your client?" Gemma glanced at Damon. "Do I need a lawyer?"

Damon set a hand on her shoulder. "No, baby. I mean, not right now. That's not why Ella's here. She just happens to be a lawyer, but more importantly, she's Robert's wife and my friend."

Ella pulled several things out of the bag and set them on the bed next to Gemma. She'd gotten far more than just panties. Bless her.

"That's a lot," Gemma commented.

Ella shrugged. "I didn't even go to a store. I keep a variety of women's clothes in my closet, just in case. You never know when someone might need some TLC." She smiled warmly.

"Whatever you see that you'd like, just take it. The rest can go back in the closet for someone else."

"That's so nice of you," Gemma murmured.

Damon was relieved that Gemma was not panicking. Maybe she did better with women than men. It made sense.

Damon considered offering to leave, but when he took a step back, Gemma grasped at his hand without looking at him. Her silent plea was heard. He squeezed her fingers and lifted them to rub against his lips.

The pile of clothes included several bras and panties with price tags on them. There were also leggings and shirts, and even a thick white sweater that looked long enough to cover Gemma.

Ella lifted a shirt. "Robert said he thought you were about my size. He was right. I bet this will fit you."

Gemma was quiet, but she wasn't hyperventilating, so that was a good sign.

Damon picked up a pair of black bikini panties. They didn't have lace or anything. Just modest cotton panties that would cover her well enough to keep him from losing his shit when he had to show Jagger her inner thigh.

He realized his issues were his and not hers. He didn't want a single fucker seeing her naked, not even his friends. He'd never felt possessive like this with a woman before. Never even thought about it for a moment.

What the hell was happening to him? At Roses and Thorns, he'd played with dozens of women over the years. They'd often been naked or almost naked. He'd never thought anything of it.

They weren't yours.

He suspected his possessiveness stemmed from a combination of factors. Partly because Gemma was the only woman he'd ever known who'd crawled under his skin and made herself at home—even if she hadn't known it.

Even three years ago, he'd gritted his teeth when she'd paraded around the pool half-naked while nearly every employee of her father could easily walk by and see her. Most of them had at one time or another. Damon was pretty certain there had been a group text among a bunch of them. If any of them had seen her sunbathing, the group had been quickly informed, and each member had found a reason to stroll by at some point.

It had infuriated Damon, but he hadn't owned her. He hadn't even fucking spoken to her. He'd needed to keep his head down and stay on task. His job had been a fucking farce. He'd really been there to spy on her damn father. Ogling the man's daughter hadn't been on the task list. It had been strictly forbidden.

Besides the possessiveness that had moved into Damon's mind and taken grip so long ago, now he was more than cognizant of what she'd been through. She'd spent the past three years paraded around naked like she was an object, and he would never fucking put her in a situation like that again.

Damon was shaking a bit as he held up the panties. "How about these?"

Gemma looked up, meeting his gaze, asking him silent questions he didn't have answers for. *Yes, I'm trembling. My mind wandered toward a dark place.*

She took the panties. "If you like them."

He shook out of his enraged state and gave her a sly grin. "I hate them. They will cover too much skin, but I want you to wear them for now, okay?"

She narrowed her gaze, but her lips were turned up. She'd caught his slight humor.

Ella ignored their banter and picked up a few bras. "Do you want to try some of these?"

Gemma glanced at the offerings and then back at Damon. "Could I just not wear a bra for now?" She shivered.

"Of course, baby. You can wear whatever you want." *Though I do wish you would wear enough to keep people from looking at anything I'd rather not share.*

It didn't appear that Gemma was going to make selections, so Damon did it for her. He reached over and picked up several items. "Come. Let's try these." He took her hand, helped her slide down from the bed, and led her to the bathroom. When he glanced over his shoulder, he said. "Give us a minute."

"Take all the time you need," Ella said.

Damon didn't care much if Gemma got naked in front of Ella, but he didn't know how Gemma felt, so he thought this might be easier. As soon as he shut the door, he cupped her face with his free hand. "You okay?"

She nodded. "I think so."

He was beyond relieved she wasn't calling him Sir, and especially not Master. He hoped that meant they were making progress and more of Gemma was taking over. He also hoped she wouldn't slide into her slave role in front of the men. If she did, he would remove her immediately and figure out some other way to accomplish what he needed.

"Would you like me to help you?" he asked.

"Yes, please," she whispered.

He set the pile on the counter and lifted his T-shirt over her head. Forcing himself not to linger on her body, he squatted down to help her step into the panties before pulling them up her legs.

She stared at them, breathing heavily. "Feels weird."

He kissed her. Maybe that would distract her. "I bet you'll remember what it feels like in no time."

She nodded and lifted her arms for him when he held up a plain white T-shirt. It fit her perfectly, much better than the ones she'd been wearing of his. Her nipples were obvious, so she'd have to wear the sweater, but the cotton shirt would hopefully keep her skin from feeling irritated by the cable knit.

After helping her into the leggings, he pulled the white sweater onto her last. "Perfect."

She took a deep breath. "Still feels weird."

"I know, but I can't have you wandering around almost naked in front of people, baby. Okay?"

She grabbed the front of his shirt and leaned in closer, tipping her head back. Was she grinning? "This isn't about me so much as it's about you, is it?"

He chuckled. "Touché."

"You don't like anyone seeing me," she confirmed.

He winced and grabbed her biceps. "No, I don't. Not because you aren't perfect but because I don't feel like sharing."

She rose onto her tiptoes and kissed him. "Do you want me to wear a bra? I can try."

"No, baby. This is fine. Just don't take the sweater off." He lifted a brow.

She nodded. "I won't."

"I need to talk to Robert now, baby. Do you want to stay up here with Ella or come down with me?"

"With you. Is that okay?"

"Of course."

"I was nervous while you were downstairs."

"Okay. You'll stay with me. But I'll warn you, some things we're going to discuss might be more than you're ready to handle." He was concerned about how she would react when she realized his intentions. No fucking way was Master J or anyone she'd ever come in contact with going to get away with this.

"I'll be okay."

We'll see.

He kissed her again and opened the bathroom door.

Ella was holding a pair of cute white tennis shoes and socks. "Maybe these will fit? Are you an eight?"

Gemma frowned for a moment. "I think so." She padded over to the bed and took the shoes from Ella before sitting down to put them on. She smiled as soon as the first shoe was on. "I guess I'm an eight."

"Perfect. That I had to totally guess blindly."

"Let's go downstairs," Damon said.

Shit. They'd taken so long Jagger was probably there by now.

CHAPTER SIXTEEN

Damon held Gemma's hand firmly in his as they descended the stairs, and he tucked her close to his side as they entered the kitchen. Sure enough, Jagger had also arrived. He and Robert were sitting on stools at the kitchen island. They each had a cup of coffee in front of them. Not something harder.

Jagger rose to his feet, his brow furrowed in confusion. Most likely Robert hadn't said a word to Jagger about Gemma.

Damon held Gemma against his side as Ella slid by them to join Robert.

With his hand on her back, Damon introduced her. "Gemma, this is Jagger. Jagger, Gemma."

She didn't lift her gaze, and she was rigid beside him. Apparently, her paralysis extended only to men. She'd done much better with Ella, but Damon wasn't surprised.

He tipped her head back with a finger under her chin, encouraging her to look at him. When she met his gaze, he spoke. "Friends, remember? You may look everyone in the eye here, Gemma."

"I'm not all that exciting to look at anyway," Jagger joked.

Damon grinned, still holding Gemma's gaze. "He lies. Maybe you shouldn't look at him. You might decide he's more handsome than me."

She narrowed her eyes. "Don't be ridiculous."

He chuckled, but he didn't pressure her further. At least she wasn't in a complete panic. "Come." He led her to the other side of the island and lifted her onto a stool. Damon remained standing, keeping one arm around her as he set his phone on the island.

"You're freaking me out," Jagger stated. "Tell me what's going on and why I'm here."

Damon would rather have this conversation without Gemma listening, but leaving her alone somewhere would be worse than having her hear what he had to say.

Damon looked at Jagger. He needed to catch him up first. He hadn't told him a thing because he hadn't wanted to risk Jagger telling his boss, which could have led to the FBI ruining Damon's chances of getting Gemma to safety.

Selfish? Maybe, but he didn't give a single fuck.

Evidently, Robert hadn't mentioned a word of what was going on to Jagger while the rest of them had been upstairs.

Damon took a breath.

"Wait…" Jagger's eyes widened and swung to the woman pressed against his side. "Gemma? As in Gemma Romano?"

"Yes."

"The woman who disappeared after the raid on her father's compound?"

"That's the one." Damon rubbed her back, trying to keep her calm.

"How…?"

Damon tugged a stool over and sat on it right up against Gemma's side, spreading his legs to keep her between them to make her feel as safe as possible. "Whoever abducted her that day sold her or turned her over to human traffickers," he began.

Jagger didn't move a muscle. He didn't even blink. His eyes were wide with shock.

"I spent three years looking for her, and two weeks ago I got a hit."

"You never told me this," Jagger pointed out.

Damon nodded. "It was always a long shot, but I never gave up."

"Do I want to know where and how you found her?" Jagger asked.

"Dark web. I bought her."

"You fucking did *what*?" Jagger shouted. He rubbed his temples with one hand.

Gemma flinched.

Damon leaned an elbow on the island and looked at his friend. "I need you to calm down and listen to me. Gemma has been held against her will and trained as a fucking sex slave for three years. I haven't even had her for twenty-four hours yet. She's barely holding it together. She's confused and struggling to find herself. I'm sorry I didn't tell you what I was doing, but it's done, and I need your help. Please try not to freak her out any more than she already is."

Jagger took a deep breath and nodded.

Damon continued, "Yes, I bought her. It was the only hope I had of rescuing her. This fucker runs a very tight ship. I'll happily give you all the information I have, but you won't find a damn thing at the pickup location. He's too good to have left anything behind. I bet by now even the dust looks like it wasn't unsettled."

Jagger rubbed his temples again. "You can't just fucking buy people, Damon, and you know it," he gritted out.

"It's done. Arrest me."

Jagger's shoulders slumped.

Gemma gasped and tipped her head back. "What?" She finally turned her gaze to Jagger. "Are you going to arrest him?"

Jagger's face flushed under her intense scrutiny. "No."

Damon was impressed by her fierceness in the face of this shitstorm. She may have spent most of the past day trembling and nervous, but she had a momma-bear side when it came to him, and frankly, he felt proud and a bit pleased.

She was trembling as she turned her gaze back to Damon. "He's right, isn't he? You could get in trouble. You can't buy people. That's as bad as selling them."

"Trust me," Jagger interjected. "An exception would be made in the case of a rescue. It would be sort of like paying the ransom money to get a loved one back. Not recommended, but sometimes efficient."

Her brows furrowed. She didn't fully trust Jagger.

Jagger looked back toward Damon. "I can't believe you didn't tell me."

Damon lifted a brow. "What would you have done?"

"Sent a thousand agents to the location, surrounded the area, and arrested everyone involved." His voice rose again.

Damon nodded. "And that's why I didn't tell you. There wasn't a chance in hell I was going to risk not making the transaction. Not for any reason. My goal was to get Gemma back. When she's able to give us details, I'll do everything I can to help provide information, but there wasn't a fucking chance in hell I was going to alert the FBI about my plans." He shot Jagger a glare, daring him to argue his reasoning.

Jagger groaned. "I hear you, but fuck."

Yeah, that about sums it up.

Damon grimaced. "Now, can you please calm the fuck down? I have two pressing problems, and then we can come back to what to do about the trafficker. Oh, and you need to have a woman in your department sit down with Gemma.

She's relatively calm around women, or at least Ella. Men make her panic."

"Okay. I can do that," Jagger stated calmly.

"Tell us the most pressing issues," Robert urged.

"Okay. Let me start with Robert."

"Oh, these problems involve us?" Robert sat up straighter.

"Yes. Whoever is abducting and training slaves is marking them with a distinct tattoo discreetly and painfully placed on their inner thighs."

Everyone cringed.

Gemma pressed her head against Damon's shoulder, her gaze on his phone in front of them on the island. She knew the pictures were in there. At least this part wouldn't be a surprise.

Damon opened the phone to the best shot he'd taken and slid it across the island toward Robert, though Jagger leaned over to look also. As did Ella.

Robert gasped. "Are you fucking kidding me?"

"I wish," Damon responded.

Robert picked up the phone and held it closer, using his fingers to zoom in tighter. "How the fuck is this possible?"

Ella sucked in a breath.

"I don't know," Damon stated. "But I'm concerned." He didn't need to tell anyone why he was concerned. They would all understand.

"That's my fucking logo," he muttered to himself. "I own the trademark."

They all knew that. And it would be impossible to say where this asshole got the logo. It wouldn't have been hard. He didn't have to get it from the artist. He could have lifted it right off the website. It was distinct though. There was no denying it was the exact same logo.

Robert handed the phone back and ran a hand through his

hair. "Do you think he's trying to connect me to his fucking crimes?"

"It kind of looks that way," Jagger agreed.

Ella looked like she was going to be sick, but she grabbed Robert's hand and didn't let go. She also didn't say anything. What was there to say? This situation was fucked up.

Jagger looked back and forth between them. "Is it possible you know this guy, Robert?"

"Or maybe your father did?" Damon suggested. Though he'd thought about this already. If Robert's father had known the asshole trafficking women, there was a good chance Damon's father had, too. And so had Gemma's.

"How the fuck would I know?" Robert groaned. "I barely knew my father at all. I mostly avoided him until after he fucking died."

Jagger glanced at Gemma.

Damon knew what he was thinking. They were going to have to grill her for as much information as possible. And soon.

"What's your other problem?" Jagger asked.

Damon wrapped his arm tighter around Gemma. He hadn't told her this. "I think there's a chip of some sort implanted under her skin beneath the tattoo."

Jagger rubbed his face, breathing heavily. "Jesus," he muttered.

"Could it be a tracking device?" Damon asked. That was his first concern. "I know that wouldn't be easy, but is there any technology advanced enough for such a thing?"

Gemma covered her face with one hand, her body stiff.

"How long ago was it implanted?" Jagger asked.

"She thinks it's been about a month."

"Then no. It can't be tracking her."

Damon blew out a long breath. He'd been freaking out over the possibility that the seller was tracking Gemma and therefore knew where she was and could easily figure out who had purchased her.

Jagger was shaking his head. "I don't know of anyone with that kind of technology. Dozens of people are working on developing it, but they haven't made it work yet, and it's unlikely this guy could've gotten his hands on anything that sophisticated even if it did exist."

"Why doesn't it exist? I thought it did," Robert questioned.

"Because it needs a battery. You can drop a device under a car, and it will last hours or maybe even days if the battery is large enough, but a tiny chip inside the human body can't hold a large enough battery. It would have to be a few inches long just to last through the day, and he would have had to implant it yesterday. It would've died by now," Jagger explained.

"Then what else could it be?"

"Is it close to the surface? Can you tell how large it is?"

"I didn't want to prod her too much. It's painful. What caught my attention is that she complained that the tattoo hurts. It shouldn't, and it looks fully healed. No swelling. No redness. No infection. When I press on it, she winces, and I think something hard is under the skin. It's not large."

"Maybe like a grain of rice?" Jagger asked.

"I'm not sure. Maybe."

"It could simply be a chip with information on it. Like the kind used for pets."

"Why the fuck would he do that?" Damon asked, trying not to lose his temper.

Gemma was shaking again.

"Perhaps it was psychological."

"But she didn't know about it. No one told her," Damon pointed out.

"It's also possible he's just batshit crazy and likes to mark his victims," Jagger stated. "Can I see it?"

Damon shook his head. "No. Can you detect it with your device without her taking off her clothes?"

"Probably. As long as she's not wearing anything metal."

"She's not."

"Do you have anything else in your body, Gemma?" Jagger asked. "Like pins from a broken bone or plates?"

She shook her head. She was fidgeting nervously.

Jagger glanced around. "Can you sit on the kitchen table for me, Gemma?"

Damon lifted her up and carried her to the table, setting her on the edge. She looked like she was going to hyperventilate.

Jagger grabbed his bag from the floor and opened it up to pull out the EFT meter. It was a small handheld device. He held it up for Gemma to see. "It won't hurt. Have you ever seen a metal detector at the beach?"

She nodded.

"It's kind of like that. It's just going to beep if it detects something metal, then we'll know."

"Okay."

"Can you show me where it is?"

She lifted her leg, and Damon helped her angle her knee out and to the side. He hated making her do this. He wanted to vomit. She was gripping his hand so hard she was cutting off the circulation, but he sure as fuck wasn't going to say a word.

Damon pushed her sweater up above the location and pointed to the approximate spot on her inner thigh.

Jagger turned on the device and eased it up her leg. When he reached the area of the tattoo, the machine beeped.

Everyone stiffened. Damon could hear the collective gasps and feel the tension in the air.

Gemma shook her head. "Get it out." She jerked her gaze to Damon. "Please, get it out."

He wrapped an arm around her and held her close, shifting his attention to Jagger.

Jagger took a seat so that his face was lower than Gemma's. Bless him. He looked up at her. "We can get it out, Gemma. I promise. But let me reassure you there is very little chance it's useful to anyone unless they know it's there and they're standing close enough to scan you. And even then, the only information it probably holds is an ID number that correlates to information held in a database. Only the person who has that database would be able to read it."

She whimpered. "I want it out."

"Okay." Damon kissed the top of her head then looked at Jagger. "How do we do that?"

"I can arrange for a doctor to do it. We'll need a field agent there to take possession of it."

"Could both of those people be women?" Damon asked.

"Yes, and I'd have someone do a thorough scan to make sure there are no other devices."

"Set it up," Damon said.

"Okay. I'll make some calls. But Damon, she needs to be questioned," Jagger pointed out. "Extensively."

"I know."

"I'll set that up for Monday, okay? I don't want to wait any longer." He turned toward Gemma again. "I can't fathom what you've been through, but the sooner someone takes down the information, the more accurate it will be. You don't want this to happen to anyone else."

Damon gritted his teeth. He hated Jagger using that line on her. It was true, but he still hated the guilt trip.

Gemma shook her head. "I'll tell them everything I know." She looked at Damon. "I will. I can do it."

He stroked her hair. "I know you can." Damn, she was brave.

Jagger stood and tucked the meter back into his bag. He

set a hand on Damon's arm. "I'm glad you found her." His mouth was still open. He undoubtedly wanted to say more, but he wouldn't. Not here. Not now. Not in front of Gemma.

Jagger turned toward Robert. "Someone is going to want to question you, too."

Robert nodded. "I should hope so."

Ella was still looking a bit green. Damon couldn't blame her. It would be disastrous if Robert was somehow implicated in human trafficking. Thank God, she was a lawyer. At least she would have an idea what they should do.

Damon helped Gemma slide to the floor, and she went with him as he walked everyone to the front door. "Thank you for coming. I know this isn't something either of you want on your plates."

Jagger frowned. "We're friends, Damon. I'm always here for you."

"Same goes," Robert added. "And it would seem you've coincidentally stumbled upon a problem that involves me. Who knows what might have happened if you hadn't noticed that logo."

Damon nodded as he let the three of them out. "Ella, thank you for everything."

"You're welcome. Any time." She touched Gemma's shoulder. "If you need anything, please call. Damon can give you my number, even if it's just to talk to a woman. Okay?"

"Thank you," Gemma murmured.

As soon as they were gone and Damon had shut the door, he led Gemma to the couch and sat, pulling her onto his lap. There were a million things going through his head, but he needed to hold her for a while. Or forever.

CHAPTER SEVENTEEN

The following morning began similarly to the previous, with Gemma waking up in a panic, confused and darting her gaze around.

Damon was grateful that she'd managed to sleep for several hours. Both of them had. And though he knew she would probably wake up disoriented for a long time to come, at least the second day was slightly better than the first. She was quicker to recognize him and her surroundings.

Damon had left all the blinds open and a light on just in case she woke up in the night. Even when she slept during the day, he didn't want her to panic.

Damon knew that among the multitude of problems he was facing, one of the urgent ones at the top of the list was the fact that Gemma couldn't stand to be separated from him. Not even across the room. She preferred to be touching him.

He was afraid her reliance wasn't healthy. Hell, nothing about any of this was healthy. He was fucking dominating her because she was only calm when he did. If anyone knew he was spanking her more than once a day, they would lose their minds. And if they knew he was stroking her to orgasm after he spanked her…

Her clothes were delivered in the middle of the morning, and it was a challenge helping her try them on to see what fit and what she liked. He'd never dressed a woman before. He'd undressed a lot of them, but not the other way around.

The problem was Gemma was reluctant and uninterested, but he needed her to have clothes on tomorrow to meet with the FBI. He didn't care what she wore. He wasn't particular about that kind of thing as long as she was happy. However, he did want her covered…and comfortable.

And happy.

And well-adjusted.

And so many other things that had nothing to do with clothes but nevertheless kept coming to mind.

Putting a bra on another person was interesting, and challenging. Actually, every part of the clothing battle was interesting and challenging. The problem was she didn't care if she was naked in front of him. At the same time, she had no fucking clue how damn gorgeous she was.

Her body was perfection. His cock was always hard because her damn tits were mouthwatering. And she didn't know or care.

Three years ago, she'd known. She'd flaunted her assets in front of God and everyone. But she'd either lost interest or modesty. It was like her emotional spectrum was off-kilter. Not right and wrong. The ability to care was gone.

He tried to add humor while he dressed her, chuckling as he adjusted three different bras to try to get the right fit. He liked the way she giggled when he laughed, but she didn't pay close attention to the way her breasts nestled in the cups.

As soon as he removed the third one, she leaned her naked body into him, tipped her head back, and made her usual request. "Spank me and fuck me."

He groaned, his hands running up and down her biceps. His cock jumped to attention. Any man on earth would salivate to have their woman ask them to spank them and fuck them. And he didn't mind doing so. Not fucking her with his cock of course. He wasn't willing to take his pants off under any circumstances.

The problem was he was worried about her emotional health. Spanking was becoming a bargaining tool.

Try on these clothes, and I'll reward you with my palm on your ass.

Pee alone in the bathroom, and I'll suck your clit until you come.

This couldn't be healthy.

He needed help. This kind of help would come from Robert. Or perhaps Colin Wynne, the owner of the Denver branch of Club Zodiac. Damon had no experience with this kind of submissive. None of his friends did either. No one he knew had ever bought a slave and set her free after three years of captivity.

He was alone in this deep water. He could ask for advice, but he didn't think anyone could possibly put themselves in his shoes.

He wondered if maybe Ella could help. She was new to BDSM, but she wasn't new to trauma. She'd had clients with all kinds of stories, some more horrific than others. Maybe she could at least understand Gemma better.

Damon shook the musing from his head as he realized Gemma was still pressing against him, holding on to the front of his shirt, her eyes pleading. Her lip was trembling too, making him aware of the fact that she'd been waiting for him to respond long enough that she'd started to doubt him.

"You said…" she muttered.

He squeezed her shoulders and leaned down to kiss her lips. "Of course, I'll spank you. Did you pick out which things you want to keep and which we should return?"

She shook her head. "I wasn't paying attention. You only said I had to try everything on, and I did."

He chuckled. "Guess I wasn't specific enough." How was he supposed to know she would actually go through the motions of trying on all these clothes without caring even the tiniest bit about what fit and what didn't?

Damon glanced at the discarded pile on the edge of the bed and sighed. He was going to have to use his own judgment. "Lean over the side of the bed, baby," he ordered as he stepped toward the clothes and began to make two piles.

"Damon…" she whined as she stretched her body over the side of the mattress, her arms above her head, her fucking sexy ass pushed out. It was still pink from earlier today when he'd bargained with her to sit on a stool in the kitchen while he'd made breakfast, an attempt to put a few feet between them.

She had still been able to see him at all times, but she hadn't been touching him. It had made her restless, but he thought it was a good assignment. Hopefully, she could sit more calmly with each consecutive meal. Eventually, she needed to be able to stay in a room alone without him.

When would that happen?

He smiled at her. "Be good, you naughty imp. Let me finish choosing what we're going to keep and what's going back to the store."

She pushed out her lip in the most adorable pout.

Damon took his time. This seemed like a good lesson, too. Patience. When she started squirming, he shot her a firm look, eyes narrowed. "Stay still. If you wiggle around, I'm going to cut your spanking short."

Her eyes widened, and she pursed her lips, freezing in place.

This is so fucked up.

Damon made his piles, choosing the bras he thought fit

best and the panties he personally liked best. All the clothes fit except for a few pairs of pants, and soon he had two piles, one of which he tucked back into the shopping bag.

Finally, he came to her side and set a hand on the small of her back. "Good girl. Ten hard swats or twenty that build in pressure?" He'd started giving her choices. Forcing her to make decisions, even if most of them were related to how she got spanked and how she came.

"Ten hard please, Sir."

He wasn't sure how the hell she'd figured out when it was appropriate to call him Sir and when it wasn't, but she'd nailed it, and he'd stopped commenting. If she wanted to call him Sir while he was spanking her, he would let her. Using the formal honorific in public wouldn't be in their best interest.

He settled his hand on her warm bottom, still pink from that morning. Somehow the little imp had weaseled two spankings out of him before noon. That was why he wasn't going to give her more than ten harder swats. He couldn't spank her all the way into subspace several times a day. *That* he was certain wouldn't be healthy. Plus, his arm and hand would get sore.

Without hesitation, he swatted her sexy ass hard enough to make her breath hitch as she rose onto her toes. She also emitted a long, satisfied moan.

"Spread your legs, baby," he ordered. He loved the way she quickly complied.

After he gave her nine more solid slaps, covering her entire bottom, he stopped and rubbed the skin.

Gemma groaned. "Please keep going."

Damon leaned over to look her in the eye and shook his head. "Ten is all you get right now."

She stuck that cute pink tongue out to lick her lips. "But I like it when you spank me," she whined.

Keeping his gaze on hers, he slid his hand down between her legs and found her soaking wet folds.

She gasped and lifted onto her toes again.

"You like it when I finger you, too," he pointed out before removing his fingers and shoving upright. He lifted her off the edge of the mattress and turned her around to set her down facing him.

"Why did you stop?" she asked, squirming against the mattress, partly because her butt was heated and probably burned but also because she needed release.

"New rules," he stated.

She frowned.

"From now on, spankings are rewards. Not punishments."

"Duh..."

That single syllable was so youthful and drawn out that Damon laughed. She'd sounded every bit like the twenty-year-old he'd last seen. She'd probably used that term with rolling eyes and hands on hips when she'd been arguing her point back then.

"You're laughing at me," she accused.

"Duh," he responded, lifting a brow. "You make it so easy." He shoved her onto her back, grabbed her hands and threaded their fingers together alongside her head. "If I continue to spank you for misbehaving, my hand will hurt. You'll manipulate everything we do to ensure you get your bottom spanked. So, yes, we have a new rule. You have to accomplish tasks to get rewards."

Now, she rolled her eyes, and he grinned. "There she is. There's the woman I remember." He bent closer and kissed her lips.

"Are you going to let me come?" she asked, breathing heavily.

He rose off her. "Yep. I'm going to watch." It was going to

kill him too, but she needed to start masturbating. Another oddity in the upside-down world they lived in.

She lifted onto her elbows, blinking. "No. I can't..."

"You can. I want to watch." He'd rather strip off his jeans and fuck her through the headboard, but instead he'd watch her fucking masturbate.

He needed to be recommended for sainthood. Not only was he keeping his cock tucked in his pants, but he never even had a moment alone to take care of the blue balls.

He needed to fix that. "After you come for me, you're going to take a nap while I shower."

She frowned. "I'll shower with you."

He shook his head. "Nope. You'll stay in this bed under the covers and rest." He hated the way she started trembling with nerves. She was growing more attached to him instead of less.

To bring her back to center and help her get started, he spread her legs and lowered his mouth to her pussy. After a quick lick and suck, which instantly made her moan, he eased back, grabbed her hand, and brought it to her core. "Touch yourself, baby." He pressed her fingers against her clit to emphasize his intent.

She was shaking, but she didn't remove her hand as he leaned back and released her. Her fingers slowly stroked around her clit.

Jesus. He was going to come.

She whimpered. "Damon..."

"I want to watch you come, baby," he stated firmly. She seemed to respond better when she felt like she'd been given a command, as fucked up as that was.

Gemma was submissive. She probably would have been no matter what had happened to her. She responded best when he ordered her than when he opted to simply make a request. Her body jumped to attention. Her nipples stiffened. Her pussy grew wet. He could actually see it since she was often naked.

"That's a good girl," he praised when she flicked her clit. "Press your fingers into your pussy and draw out the wetness." As if that were necessary.

She obeyed him though, and fuck him, but her mouth fell open and her other hand went to her breast.

"Pinch that swollen clit for me, Gemma."

She immediately did as she was told, which was hotter than fuck all by itself.

Damon wasn't going to make it to the shower. His cock was literally going to revolt behind his fly. He leaned against the edge of the bed between her legs to put pressure on it, not taking his gaze off her.

Gemma arched her head back as she went into her mind, her eyes fluttering closed. She pinched and pulled on her nipple with one hand while she flicked her clit with the other.

Fuck. Me.

Damon had never seen anything so erotic in his life. He'd never even imagined such a thing. It scared him to death because he was so fucking enamored with her. He was wrapped firmly around her pinky. And it wasn't right. He needed to help her heal and ensure she made her own choices in life. He couldn't simply take over her world and force it to revolve around him. It would be like trading one prison for another. How would she ever know what she truly wanted in life if her only decent experience was with him?

Gemma sucked in a sharp breath and then moaned loudly as she pressed her fingers flat against her clit. Her body pulsed with her orgasm, her entire frame shaking against the bed.

And Damon was about to faint because he could hardly stand upright anymore. He was panting to get more oxygen as if he'd just worked out instead of watching his girl masturbate.

When she was done, she had the cutest grin on her face, and he lifted her fingers to his mouth to suck each of them clean of her juices, one by one.

She watched him, her cheeks flushed, her legs wide. She had no modesty. And that was fine, as long as she learned to reserve it for him.

Or whoever she ended up with.

That last thought made his jaw clench. There would be no other man.

And yet, who the fuck did he think he was?

He bent over her to kiss her lips. "So sexy, baby. Thank you." She was limp as he helped her turn so that she was right in the bed, and then he pulled the covers over her. "Sleep, Gemma."

She pulled her hands out from under the covers. "Will you restrain me?"

He shook his head. "No, baby. It's not safe. Not physically or emotionally. Besides the psychological damage of being abused so badly, no one should be cuffed to the bedposts and left alone. You wouldn't be able to escape if there was an emergency."

She drew in a breath. "I hadn't thought of it like that."

"Well, now you have. What if I got in the shower and then the lamp fell over and started a fire?"

She shuddered as she stared at the lamp. "Could you maybe turn it off, just in case?"

He reached over and did just that. "Better?" He'd replaced one fear with another. He wasn't winning this battle or this war.

She nodded, but she set her arms above her head on the pillow, spread out in the position she'd said she was often tethered. *Mother-fucking prick.*

"I need to shower and shave. If you're good and stay right here while I do that, I'll reward you."

179

She smiled. "I'll be good."

He was going to need a better reward system. He couldn't continue to spank her all day, every day. Nor could he suck her pussy dozens of times. Hell, watching her get herself off had been worse than doing it himself.

She squirmed under the covers as if she were thinking about his reward. Her legs spread, again in the position in which she'd been restrained. He figured she intended to pretend.

At the last second, he had another idea. "You're pretty fidgety for a woman who just had a beautiful orgasm. Are you not fully satisfied?"

She shook her head, her cheeks pinkening further.

"You have permission to give yourself another orgasm while I shower, as long as you stay in this bed, understood?" He added that last part in his stern voice, hoping it sounded like an order.

"I..." She licked her lips. "I don't think..." Her hands fisted on the pillow as if she were fighting two opposing orders, and she was. Master J's rule that she not touch herself was at war with Damon's new proclamation that she must.

"Who's in charge of the rules?" he asked, his brows furrowed.

"You are, Sir."

"Me? Are you sure?" he challenged.

"Yes. Of course." She looked confused. *Good.*

"Are you going to obey me or Master J?"

She gasped. "You. Always."

"Did I tell you not to touch yourself?"

"No..."

"Are you still horny?"

"Yes," she whispered.

"Do you think you should lie there and let Master J control you, or listen to me and masturbate until you're content?"

"You, Sir," she murmured.

"Good girl." He leaned over to kiss her again. "Then how about you bring those hands under the covers and satisfy that pussy while I shower instead of listening to Master J in the back of your head. He's not here. I am."

"Yes, Sir." She drew her hands slowly under the covers.

He kissed her yet again and then turned and headed for the bathroom. He was so fucking tense, his entire body hurt. He shut the bathroom door, but didn't lock it. After turning on the shower, he stripped his clothes off and stepped inside.

It didn't matter if the water wasn't fully heated yet. He'd be able to stroke his cock to completion in freezing arctic waters at this point. Propping his forearm against the wall, he closed his eyes, gripped his cock, and pictured Gemma on the other side of the door, playing with her fucking sexy pussy.

CHAPTER EIGHTEEN

Gemma stared at the bathroom door for several seconds, her heart racing, her mind torn. She'd just given herself her first orgasm in three years. The first one at her own hands, that was.

It had been ingrained in her head that it was forbidden. Her orgasms belonged to her future Master. No one else. Definitely not herself. Ever.

But Damon *was* her future Master. He'd bought her. He owned her. And he'd told her to masturbate.

She took a deep breath, closing her eyes so she could think as her hands rested on her belly inches from her aching center. Damon had also insisted he was *not* her Master. He did *not* own her. No one did.

However, he was in charge. He'd said he was a Dominant. She liked how he controlled her. It felt right. She knew she was confused. Maybe she shouldn't like it, but she did.

When the water came on in the bathroom, Gemma let her hand slide between her legs. Her breathing increased as she touched herself. Three years without masturbating. Even though she'd just done so in front of Damon, it still felt foreign.

And even better than the first time. No one was watching her. No one was judging her. She gasped as she boldly pushed two fingers as deep as she could reach into her pussy and pressed her palm against her clit.

When she'd been younger, she'd never come this easily. For one thing, she'd always been nervous that someone would walk in on her. Even though she'd locked her bedroom door at night, she'd still worried she might get caught—and that would have been mortifying.

Now, three years later, she was hypersexualized from denial, edging, and built-up need. She didn't give a shit if Damon caught her, plus she knew he wouldn't come back out of the bathroom for a while. So, she reached for her nipple with her free hand and played with it while she stroked herself.

It didn't take long. Less than five minutes before she came hard against her palm, gasping for air. She was grinning when she finished, sated and panting. Damn that had felt good.

She wished Damon would fuck her already, but she understood his hesitation. How could she blame him? Who wanted to have sex with a woman as fucked-up as she was?

Damon had insisted several times he absolutely wanted her, and evidence in the form of a bulge he usually sported at the front of his pants suggested he was telling the truth. However, he'd made it clear that he wouldn't take her virginity while she was finding herself.

How chivalrous...and frustrating.

The shower was still running as she closed her eyes and let herself relax. She was safe. She was in Damon's secure estate. She was lying under the softest sheets in the world. The comforter was giving her the perfect amount of pressure.

For the first time in a thousand days, she curled onto her

side and slept with her hands between her breasts, breathing easier, beginning to trust that this was not a dream.

"Do I look okay?" Gemma asked Monday morning as she stepped out of the bathroom, dressed in more clothes than she'd worn collectively in forever.

"You look amazing." Damon came to her from across the room where he'd been getting dressed in his closet. He pulled her into his arms. "And I'm so proud of you for getting dressed in the bathroom alone." He kissed her.

She smiled. She was pretty impressed herself. She hadn't panicked a single time. Rather, she'd spent most of the time repeating *he's right outside the door* to herself over and over. She also hadn't shut the bathroom door, but she'd managed to pee, brush her teeth, comb her hair, and dress in jeggings and a dark purple, light-weight sweater that covered her butt.

Damon slid his hands up her back and grinned. "You managed to put the bra on."

She shrugged. "It feels weird. I might race back up here in a few minutes and take it back off if it starts annoying me."

"Fair enough. I'll consider it a win if you race up the stairs while I'm downstairs," he teased.

She sobered. "I'm sorry I'm so much work. I'm probably driving you crazy." And she didn't want that at all because she didn't want him to get tired of her and ask her to leave.

Where would she go? She had no one. Nothing. No money. No education. No job. Any friends she'd had years ago had been kind of fake. They'd been the daughters of her father's friends. They would never understand what she'd been through, and she shuddered at the thought of contacting any of them.

She had no living family. That fact had made it difficult to stay strong while she'd been in captivity. She'd known that even if she ever did manage to escape, no one would be looking for her. No one would care or want her.

Except Damon. She'd known he was not in the compound at the time of the raid. He'd been sent out to retrieve the damn movie she'd insisted on watching. It had been stupid. She couldn't even remember the title now. But there had been hundreds of times in the past three years when she'd been grateful for her bratty behavior that day. Knowing Damon hadn't been murdered with everyone else in the estate had been the only thing that had given her any hope at all that there was at least one human being alive in the world who might remember her, care about her, or against all hope, be looking for her.

It had been farfetched to think that Damon had any interest in her at all, and an even further stretch to think he would remember her. The fact that he'd looked for her was still shocking.

Nevertheless, Gemma had used thoughts of Damon to keep going and care enough to stay alive. She would close her eyes and think of his broad shoulders and sexy hair. The furrow she'd often seen between his brows. The surety in everything he did.

Now, here she was. In his home. In his arms. It scared the fuck out of her to think she could lose him if she didn't work hard to be the kind of woman he needed. She was too mousy, needy, and whiney for him. He wasn't going to put up with her pitifulness forever.

Damon hauled her closer, his palm between her shoulder blades, holding her in place. "Do not apologize for anything, Gemma. You're not ever going to drive me crazy. I don't want you to feel like you have to do or say anything to please me. You don't."

She wanted to believe him.

He slid a hand up to her neck and squeezed. "You are not a burden. Even if you're never able to leave the house, wear clothes, or use the bathroom alone, it will be my pleasure and honor to have you with me. Do you understand that?"

She shook her head. She didn't. He might think he could put up with her, but no one was that perfect.

Damon sighed. "I will spend the rest of my life making sure you have everything your heart desires, and that's not contingent on you staying with me. I would never ask you to make a commitment to me without extensive therapy to ensure you knew what you wanted. But I don't want you to waste one moment of your time worrying about how I feel. As far as I'm concerned, I won the lottery the day I met you, the day you first stepped into my line of sight and I got to see your smile for the first time."

She gasped. He remembered that day? She had committed it to a permanent spot in her mind, but it shocked her that he remembered.

He grinned. "You were wearing a white sundress and came flying out of the house to ask your father for money on the back patio where I was meeting with him. You were nineteen and so full of life. My heart stopped. I struggled to pay attention to a word your father said for the rest of that important meeting."

"That was the day he hired you," she whispered. He'd been wearing a suit because all her father's employees wore suits. She'd nearly stopped in her tracks when she'd spotted him. She'd known he was older than her, and would later find out he was twelve years older, but that had only made him sexier and more attractive. He'd exuded confidence which no boys her age did.

"Yes, and I tried my damndest to ignore you and block you out of my thoughts, but I failed miserably for the entire year. I found ways to at least torture myself with a glimpse of you every single day. And when you disappeared, a piece of my soul went with you."

She couldn't breathe.

He stroked her neck. "Nothing has changed. Not about how I feel. As far as I'm concerned, you're mine, and I never want to let you out of my sight again as long as I live."

"Damon..." Her heart was racing.

He shook his head. "But you need to do a lot of healing before you can make any decisions that involve me. You have a right to the life you were cheated out of. You never got to go away to college or party with friends. You've never had the chance to date or get your heart broken. And, baby, we haven't mentioned it much, but I know you're also grieving the loss of your father. You need to work on that, too."

A lump formed in her throat as she nodded.

Damon continued. "When you reach a place in life where you're able to make important decisions, I'll be yours if you still want me. If not, I will fully understand and let you go. I'll always be here for you. Always. A place to stay. A shoulder to cry on. Money. Anything you need."

It was a relief to hear him say all of that, even though she had trouble picturing a day when she might want to go into a separate room from him let alone walk out the door. She may have been young and a bit of a dreamer when she'd first met him, but she'd known her mind. And nothing had changed over the years. She was just as enamored with him today.

When would he trust that she was in love with him? She knew he wouldn't believe her if she said it today, but she felt it, and eventually, she hoped he would trust that she knew her mind.

"Speaking of money, you have enough to live comfortably for your entire life. I made sure of it. It's in an account with your name on it whenever you need it."

Her eyes went wide. She'd never thought of that. "Seriously? Was my father's money even...clean?"

"Plenty of it was legit, baby. Your father already had an account with your name on it. I simply made sure large chunks got transferred into it before the feds took over. It's clean. It's safe. And it's yours."

Wow. That was kind of a relief to hear. She didn't need to worry about a job or how to find a place to stay after all. That didn't mean she wanted to leave this house. She hoped she never left, but she liked knowing she wouldn't be destitute if Damon grew exasperated with her.

"Thank you." What else could she say?

He kissed her again. "We need to get downstairs. The agents from the FBI will be here any minute."

Gemma held his hand as they descended with good timing because a doorbell rang as soon as they stepped into the living room. It wasn't the same sound as she'd heard the previous times someone had arrived.

"That's the gate. Let me open it. I'll be right back." He pointed at the couch and shot her a commanding look.

She forced herself to settle on the edge of the sofa. *You can do this. He's just stepping out of sight for ten seconds.*

Sure enough, he was back in her line of sight moments later and heading toward the front door to open it. It would still be a few minutes before someone appeared at the door. He'd opened the gate to the estate to let them in, but he waited at the door instead of coming to her.

She knew he was trying to help her be more independent, and she took deep breaths, forcing her lungs to suck in oxygen and release it. She could do this. She was safe. Talking about what had happened to her was going to be hard, but she would do it. For herself. For Damon. For the other five women she'd refused to think about. For any other slaves Master J trained in the future.

Gemma flinched when Damon opened the door, but she pulled herself together and stood, rubbing her sweaty palms on her thighs as two women and Jagger entered the house.

They all shook hands at the door before Damon led them into the living room.

The woman leading was tall and slender. She wore black slacks and a white blouse. Her dark hair was pulled back in a sleek ponytail. She smiled warmly as she approached and held out her hand. "You must be Gemma."

Gemma nodded as she shook the woman's hand.

"I'm Lauren Rawlings, an FBI agent. Lauren is fine." She turned toward the other woman. "And this is Dr. Langston. She's a therapist with the FBI."

"Oh." Gemma hadn't been expecting a therapist. She glanced at Damon. Based on his raised eyebrows, he hadn't either.

The second woman smiled just as warmly as she shook Gemma's hand next. She had brown curly hair that reached below her shoulders and was pulled away from her face with a clip. Loose curls had escaped all over the place.

"Please," the woman said, "call me Carol. I hope you don't mind me coming along today. Based on what Agent Whitley told us, we were confident you'd need someone to talk to. It sounds like you've been through a lot."

"Agent Whitley?" Gemma glanced at Damon again.

Jagger stepped forward. "That's me."

"Oh."

"Please. Sit," Agent Rawlings suggested.

Gemma lowered back onto the sofa as Damon came to her and sat next to her. He took her hand, anchoring her to the earth. She was grateful.

"How is this going to work?" he asked the room at large.

Lauren sat in one of the armchairs while Carol sat at the other end of the sectional.

Jagger remained standing behind them. He said, "Lauren's going to ask you a lot of questions. It will be helpful for Carol to listen in so you don't have to repeat all that information to her later. When Lauren's done, maybe you can talk to Carol for a bit and see if you think she'd be someone you can trust to help you work through the trauma."

Gemma inhaled deeply, grasping Damon's hand. "Okay."

Jagger continued. "If you don't mind, I'd like to listen in. I'll sit off to the side so I'm not obtrusive. I won't interrupt. But if I make you uncomfortable, I can leave."

Damon glanced at Gemma. "I'd like to stay also if that's okay, but if you think you can be more open without me in the room, I'll leave as well."

Gemma shook her head. She certainly didn't want Damon to leave. Plus, she knew he wanted and needed to hear everything she was going to share. Like Lauren had suggested, Gemma didn't want to repeat herself over and over.

She gripped Damon's hand harder. "Please stay."

"Okay," he whispered. "I won't move."

Gemma glanced at Jagger next. "You can stay, too." She knew she needed to be brave. The more these people knew, the more likely they could find the man who'd held her. Though she had her doubts. She couldn't imagine she had anything to say that would give them much to go on.

Damon sat back against the cushions, easing her back with him.

She leaned into him.

Lauren set her phone on the coffee table. "I'm going to record our conversation, Gemma. I'll take notes, too, but I'll want to go back and listen to everything you say later. Okay?"

Gemma nodded.

"Let's start from the beginning..."

Gemma took a deep breath as the questions began. She explained everything, from how she'd met Damon to what she'd known about her father's business dealings, to the day she'd been abducted.

She told them how she'd been injected with something and had woken up in a dark basement, naked and strapped to a narrow cot. She'd had no idea where she was or how far away it might have been because the next time she'd left that property had been Friday, and she'd also been drugged that time.

She described the basement in great detail. The darkness, the toilet, the hose for bathing, the cots lined up where all the slaves slept as more of them had joined her. She told them how the slaves were forced to sleep, and how they were stripped of all modesty, using that toilet in front of anyone who was in the basement, always supervised.

She told them about the kennels that sat opposite the cots and how the slaves were punished by squatting inside them, ankles and wrists restrained to the corners, knees wide, butt resting between their parted legs, forehead to the floor.

She told them how many hours a day the slaves spent kneeling, standing, and lying in different positions on the cold concrete floor, training them until they could hold any number of positions for hours on end.

When she finished with the basement, she moved on to describe the upstairs. She hadn't ever gone to the second floor. It was off-limits to slaves, but she described everything she could about the first floor, including details about where pots, pans, and dishes were kept in the kitchen.

When Lauren handed her a sketch pad, she used several pages to illustrate every room and where the furniture had been placed. Lauren was able to figure out what direction the house was facing based on what Gemma knew about the time of day the sun came in the windows.

She told them about her cooking and cleaning lessons, and how many meal preps they'd memorized, though they'd never been permitted to eat a single bite of the food they'd slaved over.

Gemma took a break several times to drink from the water bottle Jagger handed her at one point when he handed everyone their own.

She explained about the ankle monitor she'd worn for three years that would set off an alarm if she got too close to the doors or windows. She described the other five women and how she only knew the flower names they'd been given— Oleander, Jasmine, Tulip, Daffodil, and Lily.

The punishment for speaking to each other hadn't been worth the effort to learn each other's real names and risk being caught using them. Since Gemma had been the first to arrive, she'd found herself in the position of having to help each new slave grasp the magnitude of their fate without getting in trouble.

There had been cameras in every corner of every room. Microphones were strategically placed around the first floor and the basement to keep the girls silent.

Gemma was surprised by how well Lauren and Carol were able to keep their expressions neutral. They sometimes winced or stiffened, but they were trained not to react harshly, and it showed. She wondered if they had much experience with people like her. She certainly hoped not.

"Would you like to take a break?" Lauren asked every once in a while.

Gemma turned her down. She wanted to get this over with. The two women, and even Jagger, were pretty good at schooling their reactions, but Damon was not. His body language next to her made her doubt the wisdom of asking him to stay. However, he needed to hear all this, too, and she needed him next to her.

Even when he gripped her too hard or let out a sound, she knew she was doing the right thing. If he'd meant what he'd said about wanting her in his life, she couldn't sugarcoat her past. Plus, she drew her strength from not just his presence but also from his obvious unease in a warped way.

Gemma told them about the party nights when the slaves would present themselves upstairs, how they'd stood for hours while men stroked their breasts and butts and even between their legs as long as they didn't penetrate or permit orgasm.

She described the men who'd come as best she could, but she couldn't give them much. The slaves hadn't been permitted to lift their gazes or look at anyone's face. She'd seen Master J more often than anyone. The other trainers who'd come and gone during the day had worn ski masks. Often, Master J had not. Though he'd insisted they not lift their gazes, Gemma could describe him well after three years of side glances.

When asked about punishments and physical abuse, she told them that, as far as she knew, every slave had been a virgin and kept that way. There had been strict rules about touching themselves. Though they'd been frequently tormented with roving hands from a trainer or Master J, they'd never been permitted to orgasm.

Her story was humiliating and embarrassing, and yet somehow, Lauren asked every question in a way that gave Gemma the strength to answer honestly and blatantly.

Lauren seemed surprised by the fact that they'd never been beaten. The kennel had been the primary method of punishment, but sometimes, they'd been left standing in the middle of the dank basement, wrists stretched above their heads in a V, forced to stand for long periods of time, exposed, cold, and shaking. Sometimes, they'd been blindfolded and then tormented in that position by a trainer who had touched them randomly with no warning, squirted water at them to keep them awake, or dragged the edge of a butterknife along their skin to make it feel like they were about to be cut.

Crying had been permitted. Screaming, talking, or begging only prolonged their agony.

How often had Gemma undergone such punishments? Several times a day for the first few months and then gradually less often as she'd stopped fighting her fate and learned that obedience was the key to her emotional survival.

It took hours, but finally, the questions were over, and Gemma slumped against Damon, burying her face in his chest as she tried to keep the tears at bay. She'd gone through a pile of tissues, but she hadn't let herself totally lose it. Perhaps part of that ability was her training.

Carol cleared her throat when they were finished and spoke for the first time. "If you don't mind, Gemma, I'd like to meet with you twice a week to help you work through your trauma. We can do that here if you'd like, or you can come to my office. If it doesn't feel like we click, I can also recommend another therapist after a few visits."

Gemma nodded. "Okay." She knew it would be hard but necessary. She needed to get her shit together if she was ever going to be worthy of Damon's love. She tipped her head back to look at him. "Can we do it here?"

"Of course." He stroked her shoulder.

The women stood.

"Shall we start Wednesday morning? Is ten good?" Carol asked.

"Ten is fine," Damon responded.

Gemma reluctantly released her grip on Damon as he stood to see everyone out. She slumped into the corner of the couch and curled into a tight ball.

When he came back, he silently lifted her into his arms and carried her upstairs. "I'd insist you eat, but I bet you need to rest first."

She nodded. "My stomach is in knots."

He deposited her on the bed, pulled off her shoes, helped her undress down to her panties, and tugged the covers over her before kissing her temple. "Sleep a while."

She wanted to ask him to stay. She wanted to ask him to spank her so hard that she'd forget what she'd talked about all morning. She wanted him to fuck her clear into tomorrow afterward. Instead, she simply nodded and closed her eyes. She was exhausted, and she knew she needed to prove to him that she could sleep without him next to her and calm herself down without being spanked.

It was huge. But she did it.

CHAPTER NINETEEN

They fell into a routine. It was like she was re-training. She had to learn to do the opposite of everything that had been repeated to her millions of times in the past three years. It helped that Damon seemed to grasp that she did better when he dominated her and turned everything into a command.

Use the bathroom without someone watching.

Sleep with your arms at your sides.

Soak in the tub without supervision.

Touch yourself in the bathtub or anywhere you want.

Stay in a room for ten, fifteen, twenty minutes alone.

Wear clothes for an hour, two hours, three.

Make eye contact when talking.

Open the back door.

Walk out onto the patio.

Stroll in the garden.

Open the front door.

Sit on the porch.

Since she'd been taught to clean and cook for him, he didn't permit her to do either. Since she'd been taught to kneel in front of him and suck him off, he didn't permit that either. Except for the night he'd rescued her, she hadn't seen or touched his cock directly.

Damon tapered the spankings down to two a day. She could have one after lunch before she napped and one at night before bed. At night, he helped her orgasm. During the day, he left her to do it alone after he exited the room.

She suspected part of the reason he stopped spanking and touching her as often was self-preservation. His face was tight and strained when he held her naked or spanked her. Some nights, he fingered her. Some nights, he sucked her pussy until she screamed.

She asked him to please take his clothes off and at least let her return the favor, but he refused, not wanting her to be triggered, since servicing him was exactly what she'd been trained to do.

Instead, he would only service her. How long could they go on like this?

On Wednesday, Carol arrived.

Gemma knew she liked her within five minutes. And that's about how long Damon stayed in the room before going upstairs and making himself scarce. She stared at the stairs as he disappeared, heart racing.

"Tell me about your relationship with Damon," Carol said to begin.

Gemma sighed and curled her legs under her where she sat in the corner of the sectional. Here, she felt relatively comfortable. She'd learned that she could survive longer in clothes if they were soft and stretchy and she left the bra off. So, she was wearing yoga pants and a black, long-sleeved T-shirt.

Carol tucked a curl behind her ear, but it didn't stay. Gemma was surprised that Carol was dressed relatively casually, and she appreciated it. Formality wasn't working for Gemma these days.

"He saved my life," Gemma said.

"He certainly did. How does that make you feel?"

"Grateful. Scared."

"Scared?"

Gemma shrugged. "He thinks he loves me, but I'm worried he won't be able to tolerate me forever. I'm never going to be whole." She was surprised how honest she was able to be.

"Has he said he loves you?"

"No, but he shows me."

Carol smiled. "That must feel nice. How does he show you?"

"He's been by my side nearly nonstop from the moment he...bought me." There was no way to sugarcoat that fact. "He does everything for me."

"He seems like an amazing man."

"He is." Gemma felt like she needed to defend him.

"Do you think you're in love with him?"

"I am. I was before I was abducted, and I still am."

Carol nodded. "Are you sleeping okay?" she asked, changing the subject.

"Sometimes. It's hard. I'm used to being restrained and unable to move when I'm in bed. Damon refuses to restrain me when I sleep."

"That seems like a good plan. It's not very safe."

"That's what he says. I know he's a Dominant though, and he probably prefers to restrain his partners normally, so I'm keeping him from doing that...and so many other things."

"What things do you think you're keeping him from?"

Gemma shrugged. "He refuses to let me call him Master or even Sir. He has rules, but they're all backward."

"Rules?" Carol sat up straighter.

"I can't function without rules. I panic and go into my head."

"That makes sense. What are Damon's rules?"

Gemma found herself chuckling. "They sound silly out loud. Things like I have to use the bathroom alone. I'm not allowed to cook or clean. I have to stay in a room by myself for a certain amount of time which increases every day. I have to open the front and back doors. I have to bathe alone and... touch myself."

Carol smiled with her brows drawn together. "He wants you to masturbate?"

Gemma shivered and rubbed her arms. "Because I wasn't permitted to before."

"Ah. Got it. It sounds like he should be a therapist. Unique methods, but you seem much better today than Monday, so they must be working. Don't you think?"

"Yeah. He's pretty strict and makes it impossible to disobey him."

"How does he do that? What are the repercussions?"

Gemma licked her lips. Was she going too far in telling this woman what Damon did for her? He'd told her to be open and honest and tell Carol everything, but did he expect her to talk about him spanking her?

Carol waited.

"He spanks me."

Carol frowned.

"It's what I want. It's...hard to explain. At first, he did it to get my attention when I wouldn't stop calling him Master, but then he realized I like being spanked too much, so he switched it up. Now, I have to do things that will help me improve and get better. If I meet my goals, then he rewards me with a spanking. It's like I need the physical reminder that I'm alive and really here and free. He said he only does so because I was never struck while in captivity, so it won't trigger me. And I like it so much that I spend all morning working hard to do my list of healthy things so I can earn a spanking." She tipped her head back and stared at the ceiling. "God, that sounds fucked up when I say it out loud."

"Actually, not really. It sounds kind of genius to me."

Gemma took deep breaths and lowered her gaze. "Really?"

"Sure. I mean it's the opposite of how you were punished in captivity. Lots of people in the fetish community enjoy release from impact play. You're not alone. Do you consider yourself submissive?"

Gemma nodded. "Yes. And I think that scares Damon. He's worried my view is warped, and that he can't treat me that way in the long run. I know he will miss it if he doesn't dominate me and, frankly, I crave it, too. Maybe that's crazy after what I've been through, but I want him to dominate me anyway. I'm calmer when he's in charge and when he gives me tasks and makes demands."

"Do you think you were submissive before you were abducted?"

"Yeah. Probably. My girlfriends and I used to lean around a laptop and read all about the fetish community. The more I learned, the more I fantasized about being dominated. And coincidentally, Damon featured in those fantasies."

"But maybe it's not a coincidence," Carol suggested.

Gemma shrugged. She couldn't see it any other way.

"If you were interested in him before you were kidnapped and vice versa, and then he spent three years looking for you, perhaps your relationship isn't as flimsy as you fear."

Gemma hadn't really expected this therapy session to end up being about Damon. She wrapped her arms around her knees and hugged herself, wincing when her shirt tugged tight against her shoulders.

"Are you uncomfortable discussing Damon?"

Gemma sighed. "Not really. I'm kind of surprised that we're talking about him, but I don't mind. What I'm uncomfortable with is wearing clothes." She chuckled sardonically.

"Ah. It must feel strange."

"Yes. I'm used to being naked all the time." Gemma shuddered. She was gradually starting to see her nudity through a new lens. As the fog cleared, she was starting to remember that humans wore clothes. She didn't think she'd ever feel vain about them again. She couldn't imagine a time when she would care about dresses, shoes, and makeup the way she used to or feel pretty and flirty and happy-go-lucky. But she was remembering the social convention.

"I can't imagine how that must have felt. You mentioned being kept in the basement a lot. I'm wondering how you didn't get hyperthermia. Did he keep it warm downstairs?"

"Not really. We were cold a lot, but after he cuffed us to the cots at night, he put a rough blanket over us. We could either lie still so it would stay in place, or squirm around and risk losing it in the night. We learned to lie very still at night."

"Gemma, that's unimaginable. I'm seriously at a loss for words. I'm also impressed by how well you seem to be doing after only five days. Though I'm worried, too. You might go through a roller-coaster. Ups and downs. Maybe you'll feel like you're more yourself some days and not others."

Gemma nodded. "That happens already. I'll feel a sort of euphoria, like all is right with the world for a few minutes or an hour. I sort of forget or block it out, and then it crashes, and I suddenly can't stand having my clothing touching me, and I need to curl up and cry or scream. I get agitated."

"Those are perfectly normal feelings. You might ride that roller coaster for months or years, but eventually, the goal will be for you to have fewer and fewer episodes where you panic. If you'll let me, I'll help you work to get to that stage."

"Thank you." Gemma really liked Carol.

"How does Damon react when you panic?"

"He's amazing. He seems to notice it right before I do, and he swoops in and holds me, helping me fight the demons."

"Does he sleep with you?"

"Yes. This time with you is the longest I've been separated from him." Gemma was feeling the strain of it, too. She was starting to fidget and feel kind of itchy, like ants were crawling on her.

"Do you have sex?" she asked gently.

Gemma shook her head. "No. He won't. He says I can't make that kind of decision. He touches me, and uh, well…"

"Gives you orgasms?" she provided as if they were discussing the weather.

"Yes," Gemma murmured, slightly embarrassed. "I had none for three years."

"Did you before you were taken?"

"Yes. Alone, I mean. Never with a man."

"Right. You told Lauren all six women were virgins—or were presumed to be so."

"That was the presumption, yes. I have no idea about the others. We didn't discuss it. We rarely discussed anything."

"Do you think your abduction was specifically targeted or a coincidental fallout from the raid?"

Gemma fidgeted again, the tag in the back of her shirt suddenly driving her crazy. "I don't know. I've always wondered."

"It occurred to me that if your abductor was only interested in virgins, he would've had some reason to believe that you were indeed a virgin. That would require some inside knowledge of the fact that you rarely left your father's estate. I'd go so far as to say he had insider information that confirmed there was very little chance you'd been with a man."

Gemma shuddered. "I've thought of that, but I'm not sure how it helps. I mean, it probably was someone my father had dealings with. Business that obviously went very bad. Bad enough for whoever abducted me to break into my father's estate, kill nearly everyone, and kidnap me. Why? Revenge against my father? He wasn't even alive to suffer the loss."

Gemma's voice had risen as she spoke, and she gave a choked sob as she finished. Tears fell. She'd fought them for the past two hours, and now they would not be stopped.

"You must miss your father terribly," Carol stated gently.

Gemma grabbed a tissue from the end table and wiped her eyes. "I do when I think of the happier times. I used to switch back and forth between missing him and being furious with him."

"Why were you mad at him?"

"Because I assumed he was involved in something illegal and dangerous, and it got him killed and me kidnapped. That made me mad."

Carol opened her mouth to speak and then hesitated, which was unusual for her. Finally, she cleared her throat. "I don't mean this to sound accusatory. I certainly don't have all the information, but…"

She glanced past Gemma as if verifying they were still alone before leaning forward and setting her elbows on her knees. "If your father was involved in something illegal, and Damon worked for him, have you ever stopped to wonder what Damon knew?"

Gemma played with the hem of her shirt around her knees. "Yes." The thought had occurred to her, but she hadn't let it linger. It was too much to ponder.

"Have you asked him?"

Gemma shook her head. "I'm afraid of the answer on so many levels."

"I can see that, but I think you deserve to know. It feels really important. Maybe he was an innocent bystander who happened to be employed by your father and had no idea anything was amiss."

"But what if Damon knew? Wouldn't that make Damon a bad person? What if he was doing something illegal and someone finds out and he gets arrested?" Her imagination was going rampant now.

She'd forced these questions to the back of her mind so far. She didn't want the answers. It scared the fuck out of her. How did Damon have so much money? It didn't appear to her that he worked at all. He'd spent the last three years looking for her. How did he have money to live off of? If Damon was a bad person like her father, then what? Could she stay with him? Could she support him or perhaps even lie for him to protect him? Questions she hadn't permitted herself to ponder flooded in now that Carol had voiced her thoughts aloud.

"I think you need to ask Damon those questions, but I see your mind working overtime with worry. I honestly don't know a thing about Damon. I'm not a field agent. I'm a psychologist. But, it's worth pointing out that he's obviously close friends with Jagger Whitley who has been with the FBI for years. I do know Jagger. It would shock me if Jagger had close friends who were criminals."

Gemma thought about Carol's words. She had a point. "He can't be a criminal," she muttered.

"I agree with you. So, ask him. Then you'll know."

Gemma stared at Carol. "Do you already know the answers to these questions and you're not telling me?"

Carol chuckled softly. "No, but I have my suspicions. I've been with the FBI for a long time. I'm pretty good at reading between the lines. Ask him. You don't need any extra stresses on your plate."

"Okay." Gemma chewed on her bottom lip. She hadn't let herself think about this mystery at all. It was like it hadn't fit into her overly crowded brain. But space was clearing up as she grew stronger and more lucid. Now, she needed to be brave.

Carol gathered her leather bag and stood. "We worked hard today. I'd like to come back Friday if that's okay?"

Gemma unfolded herself and stood on shaky legs. "Sure. That's fine." She felt drained and couldn't imagine doing this twice a week, but she also knew it was necessary.

Carol surprised Gemma by opening her arms and pulling her in for a hug. "I'm so very sorry for what you've been through. You're strong though. We will get you through this. I'm confident you can have a long and happy life."

"Thank you," Gemma whispered as she took a step back.

"You don't have to see me to the door. I can let myself out."

Gemma found a small smile. "I actually do have to walk you to the door. I have to open it and wait for you to pull away, too. If I don't, I won't get my reward."

Carol smiled as they headed for the door. "Can't say I've ever had a client in a relationship as unconventional as yours, and I will watch closely to make sure I think it's doing more good than harm, but if it feels right to you and you're making progress, then we won't question the method."

"Thanks again. I was afraid you wouldn't understand."

Carol paused at the door. "I'm not saying I fully grasp the situation. It's complicated. I'll think about it more in the coming days. But when you break it down, it makes sense, and I would never pass judgement on another person's needs as long as they aren't harming themselves or others."

Gemma opened the door and watched as Carol headed for her car then drove around the circle drive toward the gate. She didn't close it until Carol reached the gate.

When she turned around, Damon was heading toward her, smiling. "I thought I heard her car leaving. How did it go?" He pulled her into his arms as soon as she shut the door.

"It went well."

"You look drained."

"I am."

He smoothed her hair back from her face and kissed her chastely. "Would you like lunch? Or do you want to lie down first?"

"I don't think I can eat right now, but I would like you to spank me so I can relax."

"I figured that might be the case. Let's go upstairs."

Gemma knew she and Damon had a lot to discuss, but she was too tired to bring any of it up right now. Later. After she'd rested. Right now, she wanted her reward. She wanted to feel the rush she got when he peppered her bottom with his swats. The sting made her forget. It let her go into a quiet place in her head where there were no problems or concerns. It let her escape the real world.

She didn't care if it was conventional or not. Luckily, Carol didn't either. It worked, and as long as it was working, she wasn't going to suggest they stop.

CHAPTER TWENTY

Damon was surprised to find Jagger at his door on Friday afternoon. He wasn't alone either. He was with another agent. Damon had met him a few times. Boyd Lampros.

"Sorry I didn't call first," Jagger said as he and Boyd stepped inside. He glanced around. "How's Gemma?"

"Better. At least, I think so. She met with Carol again this morning, and now she's resting. Her sessions with Carol are challenging. She's always exhausted afterward."

"I'm sure. I've never worked on a single case as horrifying as hers."

"I hope not." Damon motioned toward the living room. "If you ever get a case more fucked up than this one, I don't want to hear about it." Not that Jagger would or could share.

Damon sat on the edge of the sofa.

Jagger and Boyd sat across from him in armchairs.

Jagger's brow was furrowed. "I wanted to tell you about the chip."

"Okay. Did it have something on it?"

"Yes. And you're not going to like it. *I* don't like it."

Damon stiffened.

"It says *Property of Damon Albertini*."

All the blood ran from Damon's face. "Tell me you're fucking with me."

"I wish I was."

Damon's heart was racing as he jumped to his feet and looked around, suddenly feeling like he was being watched. He ran a hand through his hair. "That's fucked up."

"I agree. That's why we're here."

"Please tell me you're going to sweep this place."

"Immediately," Jagger agreed.

Boyd was already pulling equipment out of his bag.

"Jesus," Damon muttered as he started pacing, trying to wrap his head around the many implications. "Why all the fanfare if he knew who the buyers were all along? And why would he leave my name on the chip? It's like he's left me a message."

"I have these same questions," Jagger stated as he joined Damon by the fireplace.

Boyd was already scanning the room, using high-tech equipment to search for bugs or cameras.

"Do you suppose he left his cute message inside all the women he sold that night?" Damon asked, thinking ahead.

"Hard to say. Maybe. It seems like his intention was to let you know that if you happened to find the chip, he knows who you are."

"Like a warning."

"That would be my guess," Jagger agreed.

"Do you think we're even safe here?"

"As safe as anywhere. He's obviously a powerful man. I doubt you could run from him if you tried. At least here in your home, you'll know there are no bugs in a minute."

Damon groaned. "How the fuck did he track me down. The only thing he ever had was a wire transfer. Those are secure."

"I agree. Which means he found out who bought her and input that data in the chip after the sale."

Damon had given the FBI everything he knew, including the website he'd used, the warehouse he'd gone to, and the funds paid.

A piercing scream coming from upstairs stopped Damon's heart, and he took the steps two at a time to get to Gemma. As soon as he rounded the corner to the master bedroom with Jagger on his heals, he realized what had happened.

Gemma was huddled in the corner of the room, hands over her head as if protecting herself or hiding.

Boyd was standing just inside the door, arms up, eyes wide. "I'm so sorry. I didn't know someone was in here. I scared her to death."

Damon rushed over to Gemma and squatted down next to her. Thank God, she wasn't naked this time. She was wearing leggings and a T-shirt. She was covered. "Gemma, it's me. Baby, look at me. You're okay. Boyd is with the FBI. I didn't realize he'd come upstairs, and I forgot to warn him you were up here."

She was gasping for every breath, shivering, but she lifted her head finally. Her eyes were wide with fear. Any human would have panicked in her situation. It wouldn't take a victim of abuse to freak the fuck out if they woke up and found a strange man in their bedroom.

She took a deep breath and nodded.

Damon cupped her face. "I'm sorry."

She nodded again. "I…"

"Ma'am. My apologies," Boyd stated from behind them.

"Mine too, Gemma," Jagger added. "We weren't thinking."

"I'm okay," she murmured.

Damon helped her rise from the corner, keeping an arm around her. He pulled her into his arms as soon as she was on her feet, tucking her head against his chest and rubbing her back. "I've got you. You're safe."

Fuck. He hoped she was safe. But how could he be sure? Her fucking seller knew who bought her. He still wasn't sure if this house was bugged. He had no idea if either of them was safe.

Damon led her to the bathroom and shut the door while Boyd and Jagger stepped out of the room. He wet a wash cloth and wiped her face. "Take some deep breaths for me."

She was wringing her hands together. "I'm sorry. I hate that I freaked out."

Damon shook his head. "This one isn't on you. Anyone would've panicked to wake up and find a strange man in their room, baby."

She nodded. "True. Okay."

"My fault entirely. I was talking to Jagger and didn't notice Boyd headed upstairs."

"What's he doing?"

Damon took a deep breath. "Looking for bugs."

She frowned. "Bugs?"

"Not insects. Electronic devices that might be listening to us."

Her eyes widened again. He hated scaring her, but she needed to know what was happening. Keeping secrets from her wouldn't help at all. "The FBI managed to read the information on that chip," he said gently.

She winced. "What did it say?" she whispered.

"Property of Damon Albertini."

She stared at him a moment and then gasped and stumbled backward as the implications sank in. "I thought the entire transaction was anonymous."

"Me, too."

"How does he know who you are?"

"I'm not sure, baby. He must've tracked me somehow after I picked you up."

"Why?"

"I assume it's a warning."

"Warning about what?" She stared at him in confusion.

"I don't know. But he obviously wants the buyers to know he's well aware of who we are. Probably to scare us into keeping our mouths shut."

She was breathing heavily now and rubbing her temples with both hands.

"Do you know whether the other five women were also having issues with their tattoos still hurting long after they'd been inked?"

She nodded. "We all had sensitivity. None of us had any prior tattoos to compare it to, so we just assumed it was normal, and they took a long time to heal."

Damon nodded. That answered that question.

Gemma lowered her gaze to the floor. She didn't do that very often anymore, so it was concerning. "Look at me," he urged.

She lifted her gaze and swallowed hard. "I need to ask you something."

He frowned. "Anything, baby."

"Carol encouraged me to talk to you, but I just…"

"You can talk to me about anything."

"Okay." She chewed on her bottom lip for a moment and then released it. "Do you work for the FBI? Were you working for them while you were working for my father?"

Well, shit. He'd known this day would come, but he hadn't expected her to piece that together so soon. He had no intention of keeping the secret from her, but he also knew it was complicated. "I don't work directly for the FBI. I've never been paid by them. But yes, I was what they call an informant.

I went to work for your father with the intent of turning information over to the FBI."

She blinked a few times and took a step back, crossing her arms.

Fuck.

Damon let her go and leaned against the bathroom counter. "It's complicated. That's why I haven't told you yet. But I'll tell you everything I know. Can we go downstairs?"

She lowered her gaze and thought for a moment before responding. "Yes." She wasn't pleased. That was clear. And he couldn't blame her. He'd be confused and fucking pissed if he were in her shoes.

He nodded toward the door, and she turned to leave. He followed her, feeling like there was a giant chasm between them. They rarely did anything without touching. He wasn't going to compound her stress by touching her without her permission, but it was telling that she kept her arms crossed and hadn't latched on to him.

"Let's go into the kitchen," he suggested when they hit the first floor.

She headed that direction and climbed onto a stool, hands steepled in front of her.

Damon got her a glass of water but didn't order her to drink it. He simply set it on the island in front of her.

Jagger came in behind them and froze midway into the room, glancing at Damon, eyes wide in question. He could surely feel the tension in the room.

Damon pointed at the stool across from Gemma. "I'm about to explain what I was doing working for Gemma's father."

"Oh." Jagger winced. Luckily, he was at her back, and she hadn't seen any of his expressions. He sat across from her and flattened his palms on the island.

Damon leaned against the counter at the sink, gripping the granite at his sides with both hands.

He needed to back this story up a decade. "I was twenty-five when my father mysteriously died of a heart attack. We weren't close. I'd barely had contact with him for years. My mother divorced him when I was five and we lived on the other side of Denver."

Gemma was listening intently, not moving.

Damon continued. "I went through my father's office and scrutinized everything in it when he died. He had a lot of property and money. I doubted most of it was earned legitimately, but I consolidated it, donated a lot of it to charities, bought this house for myself, and I've lived off his wealth for a decade."

Damon was grateful when Gemma relaxed her shoulders a bit.

"Robert's father died mysteriously a week before mine, and I suspect they were both killed perhaps because they knew something or stumbled upon something they shouldn't have known."

"About what?" She shuddered.

"Human trafficking."

Gemma nodded slowly, not appearing shocked.

"I abhor the idea of human trafficking, and hated that my father might have even known something, so I reentered society as his long-lost son and started building relationships with his friends."

"And my father was one of them?"

"Yes."

"You took a job working for my father in order to snoop around and see if he was doing something illegal?"

"Yes." No sense sugar-coating it.

"But you never found him to be doing anything that raised a flag. You told me that."

"True. Drugs. Laundering. The usual. But when I started working for your father, I was able to meet more people, get in deeper with the various families. It opened up possibilities."

"Do you think my father found out about the trafficking, too? That's why he was murdered?" She winced as she said that out loud. It still had to hurt, and she'd never had a chance to grieve.

"I don't know. We may never know. I'm more inclined to believe your father owed someone money and couldn't or wouldn't pay it. Your father was preoccupied and nervous. I assumed something was going to go down. I never expected the entire estate to be mowed to the ground. And I sure didn't realize you would be caught in the crosshairs and kidnapped."

She nodded slowly. "Were you feeding information to the FBI?" She shifted her gaze to Jagger.

"I touched base when I could, but there wasn't anything to share. The FBI isn't after small fish like your father. They can't win all the little battles. It wouldn't be worth it, and it would simply chase the bigger fish into deeper hiding—the man who is kidnapping and selling women."

Gemma dropped her elbows on the table and leaned her forehead against her palms. "And then he was killed and I was abducted, and you never got any answers."

"Exactly."

"Have you kept in touch with all those connections?" she asked the floor.

"No," he murmured. "I was looking for you."

Several long excruciating moments went by before Gemma finally slid off the stool and rushed toward Damon. She threw her arms around him.

Thank God. He hugged her close, rubbing her back and kissing the top of her head.

Jagger looked like he was going to tear up from his stool. He didn't say a word or move a muscle.

After a few minutes, Boyd joined them. "Well, I'm done. I found nothing. No evidence anyone has been in your home at all."

Gemma blew out a relieved breath against Damon's chest.

"That's good. Now what?" Damon asked.

Gemma tipped her head back. "Can we please get the chip out of me? I hate it. It gives me chills."

"I'll set something up," Jagger promised. "Early next week?"

"Thank you," Damon responded.

CHAPTER TWENTY-ONE

The procedure was scheduled for Tuesday morning, and Damon sat next to Gemma's gurney and held her hand as they met with the doctor who was going to remove the chip.

The doctor took about fifteen minutes explaining the relatively simple procedure and recommending anesthesia. After she looked at the area, she informed them she didn't think she could save the tattoo.

Gemma's eyes went wide. "Can you remove it?"

The doctor looked relieved. "That would be the easiest thing if you're not attached to it."

"I hate it more than anything on earth," Gemma informed her.

Damon was surprised, too. "How does that work? Doesn't it require laser treatments?"

"With a tattoo this small and in a location where no one will notice, I would recommend simply cutting out that section of skin and pulling the two sides together. I have an amazing plastic surgeon who can step in and sew it up. You probably won't even notice the scar in a few months. It will gradually fade."

Damon thought Gemma was going to jump off the bed and hug the doctor.

"Oh, thank God. Do it," she said.

"My pleasure. Makes it much easier to remove the chip if you don't want me to preserve the tattoo."

Gemma was so pleased, her nerves eased, and Damon was beyond grateful she would be asleep the entire time.

Now, he was next to her, waiting for her to wake up while stroking her forehead and holding her hand again. She'd been so brave. He was proud of her. She'd been through hell, and she was already so fucking strong and improving every day.

"Mmm," she mumbled as she finally started coming around.

"There's my brave girl." Damon smiled at her.

She returned the smile. "Did she get it?" she asked in a gravelly voice.

"Yes. And the tattoo is gone. It only took five stitches. She said you won't even know it happened in a few weeks."

She closed her eyes and grinned, squeezing his hand. "Thank you."

"Anytime." Damon was so damn relieved. Perhaps more than her. He hated that fucking tattoo on her skin, and if that chip made her feel as unnerved as it did him... It made his skin crawl.

As he stared at her, holding her gaze, his heart was so full. He wanted to tell her how he felt, but instead, he held it all back. It seemed too soon. He'd had her for ten days. It felt like a lifetime, but it was also nothing. A blip.

She had so much healing to do. It would be selfish to burden her with his feelings. His love. He didn't want her to feel pressured or think that she owed him for...anything.

She didn't owe him. She would never owe him. He wanted her to have her freedom and be able to live her life. If she wanted to walk away, he would let her go. It would hurt like hell. She was twenty-three. She had her life in front of her. He was thirty-five, and his only plans were to make her happy.

That was pretty pitiful for a life goal. For seven years, he'd spent his time trying to infiltrate the many Italian families and stop human trafficking. For the past three years, he'd focused all his attention on rescuing one woman from a life of slavery.

And he'd succeeded. She was free. She was right here next to him. Was she his?

She was looking at him like she believed that, and it made his world a better place.

"Can we go home now?" she asked gently.

Home. That sounded good. "Yes, baby."

She closed her eyes and smiled. "I feel safe there."

"I'm glad. I want you to feel safe." *And loved.* Did she feel his love?

He had a surprise for her. It had been delivered to the house while they were gone. He hoped she liked it. He prayed she would.

After signing her discharge papers, Damon helped her get dressed and let the nurse wheel her to his SUV. He lifted her into the front seat and buckled her in, being careful not to jostle her leg.

The doctor had said it was fine to walk on it and do regular light activities. Nothing too strenuous. That order had been accompanied by a raised eyebrow as the doctor glanced back and forth between them.

What the doctor didn't know was that Damon hadn't had sex with Gemma. She also didn't know that the activities they needed to put the kibosh on for a few days were even more strenuous—namely spanking her.

Gemma was going to have to give that up for several days. Damon was thinking it might be a good thing. It would give her a chance to see if she could manage without the crutch— the release.

When they got home, he pulled the SUV up to the front door in the circle drive, jumped down, and came around to her door. He unbuckled her and lifted her into his arms.

She giggled. "The doctor said I'm allowed to walk."

"Mmm. She's not here right now though, is she?" Damon teased. He kissed her when they got to the front door. "I have a surprise for you."

Her eyes went wide. "What surprise?"

"You'll see." He opened the door with one hand, while holding her against him with the other. After stepping inside, he dropped their bag on the floor and headed left.

"Where are we going?" She gripped his neck, grinning.

"The music room."

"Music room? You don't have a music room."

"I do now." He stepped into the bonus room that sat opposite the living room. It had been more of a useless alcove all the time he'd lived there. An odd space he'd had nothing to do with. He'd furnished it with a few armchairs and a small table just to fill the space.

Gemma gasped as she stared at what now sat opposite the seating area. "You bought a piano?"

"What?" he teased. "How did that get there?"

She giggled and squirmed. "Put me down."

He set her on the piano bench. "I don't know a fucking thing about pianos, but the guy at the music store told me this was the best brand."

Gemma stared at the glossy black grand piano, running her fingers over the lid that covered the keys. "I can't believe you did this." Her eyes were wet with tears when she looked up at him. "I can't believe you remembered."

He sat next to her on the edge of the bench and stroked one finger down her cheek. "How the hell could I forget how much you enjoyed playing the piano? The estate was always filled with your music. It was like a concert every time you played."

She leaned her head against his shoulder. "What if I can't play anymore?"

"I don't think it works that way. I bet it's like riding a bike."

"I don't know…"

He reached up and opened the lid, exposing the keys. "You could start with chopsticks and see how it goes," he suggested.

She looked nervous but smiled again. "What if I suck?"

"Then you'll practice until you don't suck." He lifted her fingers to his lips and kissed her knuckles. Rising, he reached for the pile of sheet music he'd purchased and set it on the stand in front of her. "I tried to remember what your favorite pieces were, but I don't think I really knew what they were even at the time. If these aren't right, we can order others."

Her fingers were trembling as she flipped through the stack. "How did you choose all these?" She glanced at him. "You had to know something. You got a lot of my favorites."

His cheeks heated as he shrugged. "I might have hummed a few things to the guy on the phone."

Her face spread into a huge grin. "Are you serious?"

He nodded.

She threw her arms around him. "That's the nicest thing anyone has ever done for me."

"Really?" he joked. "That's the nicest thing? I need to up my game."

"Well, you can't top buying me from a slave owner, but it's close."

He leaned back and met her gaze. "I'm so sorry for what you went through and how long it took me to find you. I want you to be happy. I'll do everything in my power to make that happen."

"You already have." She twisted to face him. "I want to do something for you."

"You don't need to. I have everything in the world."

She shook her head. "You don't. I know you must miss your club."

He frowned. "Not at all. I have you. That's all I need." *But, do I? Do I have her for eternity?*

"I want you to take me there," she declared.

"To Roses and Thorns?" he asked as if it weren't obvious.

"Yes. I want you to show me what you like. I want to know you better."

"I'm not sure that's a good idea."

"Why not? Are you embarrassed about me?"

He lifted both brows and gave her a pointed look. "I could never be embarrassed by you, baby. Don't think that for a moment."

"Then give me a good reason why we can't go."

"Because something there might trigger you and freak you out for one thing."

"You'd be with me, and I'll be strong enough to face other people's kinks in a controlled setting. You said everything in the club is consensual. I know the difference," she countered.

"I never want to dominate you in a way that risks upsetting you."

"You dominate me all the time, Damon. And I like it. A lot. I promise I understand the difference. You make it abundantly clear every day that I have the power. That I can say no. That I can stop whatever we're doing with one word. Red."

He was impressed by how far she'd come and how well she understood. Maybe she could manage a visit to the club. He could at least take her one day and let her see for herself. They didn't have to play. They could just visit and wander around.

"Maybe," he relented. "In a few weeks. If I think you're ready. You've made amazing progress since you got here, but you have a long way to go. Carol has told you that, right?"

"Yes, but I think I can handle a night at Roses and Thorns."

He kissed her lips briefly. "I won't rule it out, but not yet." He pointed at the piano. "Play me something." He started to stand.

She grabbed his hand. "Where are you going?"

He pointed to the armchairs. "I'm going to sit behind you right there and listen."

"Okay." She relaxed at his proclamation, but he could see her nerves creeping back in as he rose. He was definitely right about one thing. She'd come a long way, but she still had a long way to go.

The moment she started playing, Damon relaxed in the chair and watched her. He'd never been able to stand around watching her when she played. All he'd managed to do was find a reason to walk through the room some days so he could catch a glimpse of how fucking pretty she was when she played.

He remembered how her mouth would tip up in a slight smile and her brows would furrow in concentration. She would sit with her back straight and lean into the music. Watching her was half the entertainment.

She fumbled several times for a few minutes before switching the sheet music. Maybe she was looking for something easier because when she started playing again, it was beautiful.

She had to stop many times and go over a section again and again, but thirty minutes later, she had made it through about half that first piece.

Damon finally rose and returned to her, setting his hands on her shoulders.

She tipped her head back to look at him. "I'm rusty."

"You're gorgeous, and you'll get it, but right now, you need to eat something and rest. Your leg has to be sore."

"I don't think playing the piano counts as a strenuous activity, but I am hungry."

She squealed when he lifted her into his arms again.

"Are you going to carry me everywhere?"

"If you'll let me." He kissed her again when they reached the kitchen and he deposited her on a stool. "Leftover fajitas from last night?"

"Sounds delicious. Are you ever going to let me cook?"

He winced. "I don't know. We'll see, but it won't be until I get over the thought of you doing so as a slave."

CHAPTER TWENTY-TWO

Two weeks later…

"Damon?"

Damon was sitting on the edge of the bed, surrounded by piles of Gemma's clothes, a seam-ripper in his hand. He looked up as she entered the room.

She stopped in the doorway. "What are you doing?"

He held up the small tool. "Removing the tags from all of your clothes."

She frowned. "Why?"

"Because they annoy you."

She blinked at him, a slow gorgeous smile spreading across her face. "I can't believe you noticed or thought of that." She shuffled toward him, her stance changing from confusion to a sexy, coy sway.

"I notice everything, baby."

When she reached him, she took the seam ripper from his hand and set it on the nightstand before placing her hands on his shoulders. "Did you notice I had a grocery order delivered today?"

He smiled and grabbed her hips, spreading his legs and pulling her closer. "Yes." He kissed her. "And I'm proud of you for taking the initiative. Did you order anything special?"

She chewed on her bottom lip as she nodded, her hands sliding down to his pecs. "As a matter of fact…"

He squeezed her hips. "Gemma…" he warned. "What naughty plan are you plotting?"

She took a breath and lifted her gaze. "Please let me cook tonight. I want to make something special. I found the recipe online and ordered everything."

He hadn't let her lift a finger to do anything in the house yet. Not cook or clean or so much as run a load of laundry. It made him nervous. He wanted to be absolutely certain she never did anything under the guise of being his slave.

She'd changed so much in the three and a half weeks since he'd found her. Every day she'd improved. She still didn't like to be separated from him for long periods of time, but she could leave a room on her own, bathe, use the toilet, and choose her own clothes from the closet.

"I used to love cooking. It's cathartic. And I make some amazing meals. I can't spend the rest of my life roaming around your house doing nothing. Please?"

He kissed her. "Yes."

Her eyes lit up. "Really?" She smiled broadly.

"Yes. As long as you appear to be enjoying yourself, and you don't mind me hovering to make sure."

She nodded excitedly. "You can sit on the stool like you always make me do." She lifted her hands and clapped them together.

His chest tightened. Maybe he should have relented on this issue sooner. She was so enthusiastic he might have misjudged her ability to differentiate between cooking for pleasure and being his slave.

"And we're still going to Roses and Thorns tonight, right?" she asked.

"Again, yes. As long as you don't get uncomfortable or panic. If I get a single hint that you're uncomfortable, we will leave."

"Okay. I promise I'm ready. I want to see the club. I want to understand you better."

"You understand me fine, Gemma," he warned. "I've told you a hundred times being Dominant doesn't have to define me. I'm yours no matter what. I don't need anything else as long as I have you."

She licked her lips. "Are you?"

He lifted a brow. "Am I what?"

"Mine?" Her hands came back to his chest and moved up and down as she leaned closer. "Because if you really believe that, why are you still keeping your pants on?"

He stiffened. The little imp had been pressing this issue for more than a week. He'd put her off.

"I'm starting to think you don't want to have sex with me. Is that it?" she asked his chest.

He groaned. "Definitely not, baby. You're rubbing yourself against my cock right now. Does it feel like I don't want you?"

"No," she murmured, "but you're going to give me a complex. If it weren't for the fact that I've already had my mouth on your cock and I've seen the bulge in your jeans and sweats every day, I would think you weren't interested in me that way."

This time he growled. "Every inch of me is interested in you that way, Gemma."

She lifted her face. "Prove it. I'm done waiting."

He hesitated. "I won't be able to let you go if we do this, Gemma," he warned.

"I don't want you to let me go." She lowered her hands to the hem of her shirt, pulled it over her head, and tossed it onto the large pile of clothes he'd been altering.

He nearly swallowed his tongue. She wasn't wearing a bra, which wasn't unusual, but the sight of her fucking amazing tits always made him harder. He saw her naked every day, partly because she still wasn't a huge fan of clothes and partly because he suspected she'd been trying to tempt him more with every passing day.

He was done fighting this battle. She was holding his gaze without looking away. She meant it. "Please," she whispered.

Damon reached over his head with one hand and pulled his T-shirt off, tossing it aside a second later without paying any attention to where it landed.

She smiled slowly. "Yeah?"

He chuckled as he reached for the front of her jeans to unbutton and unzip them. Before he pulled them down her body, he looked her in the eye. "One of these days I'm going to ask you to marry me, and you're going to say yes, and then there won't be any question about you being mine for the rest of your life."

She grinned. "I'll look forward to it."

He tugged her jeans down but before they were past her thighs, he stood, grabbed her by the hips, and spun around to deposit her on the bed.

She giggled as he yanked off her shoes before removing the rest of her clothes. When he finally had her naked, he bent her knees, parted her legs and pressed them wide.

She fisted the comforter at her sides, already whimpering.

She was wet, and her scent was intoxicating. When he leaned down to kiss her pussy, she arched. "Damon..."

Slight stubble was growing in. He hadn't mentioned it because every time he thought about it, it infuriated him to realize she'd been waxed, which meant some twisted fuck had intimately touched his woman within a few days of him finally rescuing her.

"Damon…" she murmured.

He lifted his gaze.

"I can read your mind."

He closed his eyes. Could she?

"It's starting to itch sometimes. Will you please shave it soon?"

He flinched. "Me?"

"Yes. I can't stand the idea of someone pouring hot wax on my pussy ever again. The idea makes me cringe. And I'm afraid I'll cut myself. Will you do it?" Her cheeks were pink, and he didn't think it was from arousal this time.

"Yes, baby, if that's what you want. Or you can grow it. It doesn't matter to me."

She scrunched up her nose. "I don't think I'd like that."

"Then I'll shave it for you." He couldn't believe he was consenting to this. It would absolutely freak him out worrying he might cut her the first time, but he assumed he would get used to it and not panic after the first few times. He would certainly do anything for her. Anything in the world. If his woman wanted him to shave her pussy, then by God he would do it.

"Okay, but right now, please take your pants off."

He smirked as he released her to do her bidding. Finally, he was naked in front of her. He wrapped his hand around his cock and stroked from the base to the tip, watching her expression.

When she licked her lips, he groaned. Without shifting his gaze away from her gorgeous body, he reached toward the nightstand, pulled the drawer open, and snagged a condom.

"You don't need that, Damon," she murmured. "I'm covered for a few more months anyway. We were given birth control shots. That's why I haven't had a period either."

He hesitated. His chest rose and fell with every breath. He'd wondered but hadn't wanted to ask. "I've never had sex without a condom, Gemma."

She smiled. "Then I won't have to worry about catching anything from you."

He leaned over, set his hands on either side of her, and met her gaze. "The last time my cock was inside a woman was before I met you. I've been tested since then."

She gasped, eyes wide, mouth falling open. "Are you serious?"

He nodded. He'd never told her this, but she deserved to know. "I've been busy."

"Looking for me..."

"Yes. I couldn't stand the idea of fucking some random woman."

She swallowed hard. "That's..." She shivered. "I'm so horny, I'm going to come from your stare. Please make love to me."

He shoved the pile of clothes farther toward the foot of the bed, dragged her to the center, and climbed over her. Nestled between her legs with his cock lodged near her entrance, he kissed her senseless.

It was impossible to avoid moaning into her mouth as he devoured her. He'd kissed her many times but never like this. Never with this heat or this level of passion. He'd been afraid that if he did so he would lose control.

Gemma arched and squirmed against him, making it hard to keep from thrusting into her. He wanted her to come first though, and he finally released her lips and shifted his body down hers, pausing to suckle her nipples before moving lower.

She was panting by the time he pushed her legs open and lowered his mouth to her pussy. He didn't waste any time either. He loved when she writhed against him. He loved the way she fisted his hair and held him against her while he thrust his tongue into her as deep as he could reach.

Damon had to hold her thighs steady to keep her from wiggling out of his reach as he refocused his effort on her clit, sucking and flicking it the way he knew she liked.

He knew the moment she was about to come. Her body stiffened, and her hips arched as much as he'd let her, and then she cried out as she reached her climax. She was still pulsing, gasping, and squirming when he crawled back up her body and lodged his cock at her entrance.

"Please," she begged.

He'd visualized this many times. Every possible scenario. Fast. Slow. And everything in between. Now that the moment was here, he had to make a decision.

Gemma grabbed his hips. "Damon," she whimpered. "Do it. Just do it."

He drew in a breath and thrust into her all the way to the hilt.

She gasped. Her face scrunched up in a wince for a moment, and then she blew out a breath. Her body was tense. Her legs were shaking. "You're in me," she murmured.

He swallowed, trying not to move, wanting her to adjust first. "Very much so."

"Are you going to move?" she breathed.

"In a second. Are you okay?" He hated hurting her, and he knew he had.

"I'll be better when you move."

"I'll be coming immediately when I move," he warned her.

She grabbed his face and held his gaze. "That's the idea."

"I'd rather last a while longer, but there's not a chance. You have a death grip on me."

"I bet we can do it again in a few minutes, and you'll last longer."

He set his forehead against hers. "We can do it a million

times, baby, but I want it to be good for you. I hate hurting you."

She slid her hands to his shoulders. "It's tight, but I'm okay, Damon. You've been using three fingers in me for a while. I'm not that fragile." She lifted her lips.

He groaned. His eyes rolled back. He couldn't hold back another moment. Gritting his teeth against the need to come, he eased out and slid back in.

Gemma moaned. "Oh, God." Her fingers dug into his shoulders.

Heaven. There was no other word. Not just because it had been four years but because it was Gemma.

Damon slid almost out and thrust in deeper. He wasn't going to last. He held his breath as she writhed under him.

She was panting. "I didn't know," she breathed out. "Holy shit. That feels so good. Do it again."

How could he deny her? Damon forced himself to focus on her expression while he made love to her, trying to ignore the way his balls were drawing up and how hard his cock was.

He hadn't really expected her to enjoy it this first time, but by all appearances she was far from disappointed, so he slid a hand between them and found her clit.

She cried out again when he stroked the swollen nub. Her hips lifted as she dug her heels into the mattress. "Damon," she shouted.

He held himself deep and stroked her faster until she screamed.

God, yes. Fuck, yes.

The moment her body stiffened with her orgasm, he slid his hand out from between them, used both hands to hold her shoulders, and resumed thrusting. The pulsing of her pussy milked him, forcing him over the edge two seconds later.

He groaned around his release, filling her tight pussy with

his essence. Nothing had ever felt so good in his life. Bare. Inside the only woman he'd ever loved and would ever love.

He was the luckiest bastard on Earth.

He was panting when he found his voice. "I love you, Gemma. So much it hurts."

"I love you too, Damon." She held his gaze. She was grinning.

Suddenly, he kissed all over her face and down her neck, everywhere he could reach.

She giggled.

"I can't get enough of you," he informed her. "I'm going to yank your clothes off the moment we get home from the club and do this again. It will be better the second time. I promise."

"I don't see how that's possible, but I'm up for the challenge."

When he kissed her left shoulder, he paused and kissed it again. "This sexy mole on your shoulder was most helpful. Did you know that?"

She twisted her head to look at the spot. "How?"

"It's how I knew for sure I'd found you."

"My mole? You saw it in pictures? Didn't you recognize my face?"

He shook his head. "The seller never shared your face."

Her breath hitched. She pushed him off her and sat up. "Seriously?"

He narrowed his gaze, confused. "What's wrong?"

She smiled. "Do you know how much that means to me? That motherfucker took millions of pictures of me. I assumed my face was all over the planet by now. Do you suppose he didn't include *any* of our faces?"

Damon drew in a breath and stroked her cheek. "I can't be sure, baby, but he didn't share them with the buyers. He probably didn't want to risk anyone recognizing the girls he was selling. But I knew your body better than I should have. I didn't need your face to know it was you."

She blinked. "You'd never seen me naked."

He shrugged, not containing his grin. "Baby, the only part of you I hadn't seen was your nipples. You strutted around that damn pool in the skimpiest bikinis I've ever seen."

She slowly smiled. "And you watched."

"Fuck, yes."

She pushed him to his back and climbed over him, straddling him, her breasts swaying. "You saved my life." She leaned closer and kissed him. "I'll never be able to thank you enough."

He slid his hands up her back. "I'm so fucking glad I found you. There are no words. I'm sorry it took me so fucking long, but you're mine now."

"I was always yours."

"Yeah, you were, baby. You were." He couldn't argue that fact.

CHAPTER TWENTY-THREE

"It's like a whole different world I only knew about in books and on the internet," Gemma murmured into Damon's ear.

She hadn't let go of his arm for a single moment since they'd arrived at Roses and Thorns an hour ago. They hadn't participated in anything, but that was okay. She agreed she wasn't ready for that tonight. She was content simply observing.

What she did know was some of the scenes were titillating, and she was making a mental tally of the aspects of BDSM she would ask Damon to help her experience over time.

He was being so careful with her. Mostly, he stared at her while she watched the scenes unfolding around them.

Yeah, it was weird, but she hadn't found herself triggered. It was obvious every single thing that happened in Robert's club was consensual.

Ella was there, too. She had followed Gemma and Damon for the first thirty minutes, providing female support and answering questions. But she'd gone to Robert's office a while ago.

Jagger was there, too. He'd arrived before Damon and

Gemma. She knew he was there for another layer of moral support to ensure Gemma didn't panic. She appreciated her growing list of friends.

She was almost feeling like a normal human being for at least a fraction of every day. Each day she felt more like she might survive intact. She wasn't Marigold. She wasn't the old Gemma either. There was no going back. She was becoming a new version of herself, and she liked it.

Damon did, too. She knew because he was always smiling at her, pleased with her gradual changes.

They were watching a spanking scene, and Gemma was trying not to let herself react to the restraints holding the naked woman to the bench. She kept reminding herself the woman wanted this. She'd scheduled this scene specifically with the Dom who was swatting her red bottom. It was consensual. Safe. Sane.

Suddenly, a voice made ice crawl up Gemma's spine. She stopped dead, stiffening as all the blood ran out of her head, leaving her feeling like she might faint.

She gripped Damon's arm harder and squeezed her eyes closed. She couldn't breathe. Surely her mind was playing tricks on her.

"Gemma?" Damon whispered her name so close to her ear. "Baby, what is it?"

The voice spoke again, making her wince. She had to force herself to turn a few inches to the left, mostly to prove to herself that her mind was playing tricks on her. There was no way Master J was here at Roses and Thorns. Not a chance. It wasn't possible.

Except, there he was, two yards away from her. His back was to her. He was attaching a woman to a St. Andrew's cross. He was issuing instructions as he stretched her arms above her head and restrained her.

Gemma screamed so loud the entire room fell silent. She started shaking violently as the man spun around to face her.

Her legs gave out. She would have collapsed on the floor if Damon hadn't grabbed her around the waist.

"Fuck." Master J's eyes bugged out, and he turned and ran from the room, shoving everything and everyone out of the way.

The commotion around her was instantaneous. Shouting and running. Damon never let her go, though. He swooped her off the floor and cradled her against him as he turned in the other direction.

Gemma couldn't focus. Moments later, she felt herself fading. She knew she was going to faint, and she didn't care. She needed to escape, so she welcomed the darkness as it crept in.

"Baby..."

Gemma moaned and burrowed herself deeper against Damon's chest. She clung to his shirt, uncertain why she was asleep in his arms for several moments.

Finally, her memory rushed in, and she gasped, coming fully alert and sitting up straight in his lap. She yanked her head around to take in her surroundings. "It was him. Master J. I saw him."

"I know, baby." Damon rubbed her back. His brows were furrowed deeply with concern.

"Did he get away?"

"No. The police have him." Damon cupped her face. "They're out front, and he's in cuffs. He can't get to you. I promise. You're safe."

She thought she might hyperventilate as panic set in again.

"Deep breaths, Gemma. It's over. They've got him. He didn't even bother to deny anything. In fact, he was muttering your name under his breath while Jagger and Robert tackled him to the ground."

"My name?"

"Marigold," he whispered. "He was more shocked to see you than you were him."

She started shaking. "Why the hell was he here?"

"I don't know. I suspect he was bored after selling off his entertainment." Damon seethed. She could tell he was barely containing his anger. He was only doing it by a thread, for her sake.

Damon held her so tightly that it almost hurt. He didn't give her enough room to fully breathe. "He claims he never knew who you were, who had bought you, or where you'd been taken from, but he hadn't expected to ever see any of the women again."

"But he came to a fetish club," she pointed out. She sat up straighter. "And he knew your name. It was on the chip. He had to know you were a member here."

Damon shook his head. "I don't think he knew what was on that chip. And as far as he was concerned, you weren't sold to an upstanding, law-abiding citizen who practices consensual BDSM. He sold a slave. He probably expected you to be on the other side of the globe by now or living in some sick fucker's basement as he used you for what you were trained."

Gemma shuddered.

Damon cringed. "Sorry."

What he'd said made sense, though. The women he'd trained wouldn't show up in a legit establishment for legal fetish play.

Damon turned her so he could more fully hug her against

237

his chest. He buried his face in her hair. "I'm furious but also relieved. He can't get to you now. He'll be locked up for life. I don't have to spend the rest of my life looking over my shoulder, wondering who that fuck was and worrying he might find you."

Gemma collapsed against Damon's chest, her eyes closing. She wasn't sure how long before her mind would shut down again. She was close to another panic attack. But she understood what Damon had said. She would live through this night and be stronger and safer because of it.

Master J could never hurt her again. He also couldn't hurt anyone else.

Suddenly, Gemma had another thought. She sat up straighter, putting a few inches between her and Damon. She met his gaze and grabbed his shoulders. "You said he didn't know my real name."

Damon drew in a breath and nodded.

"Then he wasn't the one who raided my father's compound and kidnapped me."

Damon swallowed, not looking away. "No, baby. I don't think so. Not if he's telling the truth."

"Then someone else kidnapped me."

Damon set his forehead against hers and sighed. "Most likely."

Her heart was racing. "Damon…"

He nodded. "I know, baby. I know. But we have to take this small victory. That demented fuck held you for three years. He did unthinkable things to you and five other women. He can't do it again."

"But he wasn't working alone…"

Damon winced. "Human trafficking is a battle that will never be fully won, but today is a victory. The FBI will question this guy until he wishes he were dead. They'll figure out what he knows and keep working. There's always a bigger fish. One day, he'll get caught too. The FBI won't stop looking for the other women, and they won't stop looking for whoever kidnapped you."

AUTHOR'S NOTE

I hope you've enjoyed *Marigold*. The Roses and Thorns series has six full-length novels. Each novel stands alone, but they will be more enjoyable if read in order. Each of the other five women has a story to tell.

Roses and Thorns:
Marigold
Oleander
Jasmine
Tulip
Daffodil
Lily
Roses and Thorns Box Set One
Roses and Thorns Box Set Two

To learn more about Gemma and Damon, they have a novella called *Gemma's Release*. See my website for details.

If you want to know more about Robert and Ella, they are featured in a novella called *Roses and Thorns* which is published in my anthology: *Where Alphas Dominate.*

Other side characters from Roses and Thorns who will make appearances in this series are Boyd and Macy. They have a novella called *Ruined* in *Black Light: Roulette Finale.*

ALSO BY BECCA JAMESON

Shadowridge Guardians:

Steele by Pepper North

Kade by Kate Oliver

Atlas by Becca Jameson

Doc by Kate Oliver

Gabriel by Becca Jameson

Talon by Pepper North

Bear by Becca Jameson

Faust by Pepper North

Storm by Kate Oliver

Blade by Pepper North

King by Kate Oliver

Rock by Becca Jameson

Blossom Ridge:

Starting Over

Finding Peace

Building Trust

Feeling Brave

Embracing Joy

Accepting Love

Blossom Ridge Box Set One

Blossom Ridge Box Set Two

The Wanderers:

Sanctuary

Refuge

Harbor

Redeye

Nonstop

Standby

Takeoff

Jetway

Open Skies Box Set One

Open Skies Box Set Two

Shadow SEALs:

Shadow in the Desert

Shadow in the Darkness

Holt Agency:

Rescued by Becca Jameson

Unchained by KaLyn Cooper

Protected by Becca Jameson

Liberated by KaLyn Cooper

Defended by Becca Jameson

Unrestrained by KaLyn Cooper

Delta Team Three (Special Forces: Operation Alpha):

Destiny's Delta

Canyon Springs:

Caleb's Mate

Hunter's Mate

Corked and Tapped:

Volume One: Friday Night

Catching Zia

Catching Lily

Catching Ava

Spring Training Box Set

The Underground series:

Force

Clinch

Guard

Submit

Thrust

Torque

The Underground Box Set One

The Underground Box Set Two

Wolf Masters series:

Kara's Wolves

Lindsey's Wolves

Jessica's Wolves

Alyssa's Wolves

Tessa's Wolf

Rebecca's Wolves

Melinda's Wolves

Laurie's Wolves

Amanda's Wolves

Sharon's Wolves

Wolf Masters Box Set One

Wolf Masters Box Set Two

Abandoned

Betrayed

Wolf Gatherings Box Set One

Wolf Gathering Box Set Two

Durham Wolves series:

Rescue in the Smokies

Fire in the Smokies

Freedom in the Smokies

Durham Wolves Box Set

Stand Alone Books:

Blind with Love

Guarding the Truth

Out of the Smoke

Abducting His Mate

Wolf Trinity

Frostbitten

A Princess for Cale/A Princess for Cain

Severed Dreams

Where Alphas Dominate

ABOUT THE AUTHOR

Becca Jameson is a USA Today best-selling author of over 150 books. She is well-known for her Wolf Masters series, her Fight Club series, and her Surrender series. She currently lives in Houston, Texas, with her husband. Two grown kids pop in every once in a while, too! She is loving this journey and has dabbled in a variety of genres, including paranormal, sports romance, military, reverse harem, dark romance, suspense, dystopian, BDSM, and Daddy Dom.

A total night owl, Becca writes late at night, sequestering herself in her office with a glass of red wine and a bar of dark chocolate, her fingers flying across the keyboard as her characters weave their own stories.

During the day--which never starts before ten in the morning!--she can be found walking, running errands, or reading in her favorite hammock chair!

...where Alphas dominate...

Becca's Newsletter Sign-up

Join my Facebook fan group, Becca's Bibliomaniacs, for the most up-to-date information, random excerpts while I work, giveaways, and fun release parties!

Facebook Fan Group:
Becca's Bibliomaniacs

Contact Becca:
www.beccajameson.com
beccajameson4@aol.com

f facebook.com/becca.jameson.18
X x.com/beccajameson
o instagram.com/becca.jameson
BB bookbub.com/authors/becca-jameson
g goodreads.com/beccajameson
a amazon.com/author/beccajameson

Made in the USA
Columbia, SC
22 May 2024

35617882R00143